WY 1/10
JUN - - 2014

Susanna Carr has been an avid romance-reader since she read her first Harlequin Mills & Boon® Modern at the age of ten. Although romance novels were not allowed in her home, she always managed to sneak one in from the local library or from her twin sister's secret stash.

After attending college, and receiving a degree in English Literature, Susanna pursued a romance-writing career. She has written sexy contemporary romances for several publishers and her work has been honoured with awards for contemporary and sensual romance.

Susanna lives in the Pacific Northwest with her family. When she isn't writing she enjoys reading romance and connecting with readers online. Visit her website at: www.susannacarr.com

Recent titles by the same author:

A DEAL WITH BENEFITS
  (One Night with Consequences)
HER SHAMEFUL SECRET
THE TARNISHED JEWEL OF JAZAAR

Did you know these are also available as eBooks?
Visit www.millsandboon.co.uk

Dev reached out and curled his finger under her chin. Tina's skin tingled as he guided her to look directly at him. Dev was close—too close—as he leaned forward. His gaze dipped at her mouth and her lips stung with awareness.

"Whatever you're planning," he said softly, his gaze focused on her mouth, "don't."

She pursed her lips. "I have no idea what you're talking about."

"Remember the agreement," he said as he dragged his thumb along the curve of her lip. "I want—I expect—a devoted wife."

Tina frowned. Did he think she had the power to hurt him? That was laughable.

Dev's harsh features darkened and he abruptly dropped his hand. "I have several meetings and I'm late. I will see you at home tonight. Be good."

Maybe she was reading the signs incorrectly, Tina thought as she watched him walk away. She could have sworn she had seen longing in his eyes and felt a tremor in his hand. Dev didn't want her as a wife, but he still desired her.

And after everything that had happened between them Tina was ashamed that she still yearned for his touch. She hoped he would never figure that out. If that happened she would be powerless against him.

SECRETS OF A BOLLYWOOD MARRIAGE

BY
SUSANNA CARR

MILLS & BOON

Published in Great Britain 2014
by Mills & Boon, an imprint of Harlequin (UK) Limited,
Eton House, 18-24 Paradise Road, Richmond, Surrey, TW9 1SR

ISBN: 978 0 263 24200 3

Harlequin (UK) Limited's policy is to use papers that are natural,
renewable and recyclable products and made from wood grown in
sustainable forests. The logging and manufacturing processes conform
to the legal environmental regulations of the country of origin.

Printed and bound in Great Britain
by CPI Antony Rowe, Chippenham, Wiltshire

SECRETS OF A BOLLYWOOD MARRIAGE

To Sarah Stubbs,
with thanks for her editorial insights and support.

CHAPTER ONE

TINA SHARMA STOOD at the front door of her home and closed her eyes. She inhaled deeply as she allowed the hot, fragrant breeze to waft along her skin and tug at her thin shirt. She had missed the heat of the night and the familiar scent of tropical flowers. She even longed for the chaotic noise and energy of Mumbai. Once she had thought they were out of her reach forever, but she was back and no one could keep her away.

Not even her husband.

The unexpected tears stung in the back of her eyes as a sob clawed her throat. No, she decided fiercely. She wasn't going to do this. No more crying, especially over him. She had done enough of that to last a lifetime.

Her mouth trembled and her hands shook as the unpredictable emotions balled into a fiery knot in her stomach. Anger. Hate. Fear. She needed to keep it together if she was going to walk alone and unprotected into the lion's den.

Tina's eyelashes fluttered when she heard the door swing open. She had seen the luxury cars parked in the driveway and heard the loud, pulsating *bhangra* music as she had approached the house. Now she saw the men and women dancing to the primitive beat in the main hall. There was obviously a party going on.

Was it to celebrate her absence? Would the party end abruptly once she stepped inside? Perhaps that would be best, Tina decided as she pulled her gaze away from the guests. As much as she would prefer to have witnesses, she knew they would not be on her side.

"Memsahib!" the elderly manservant declared as he stood at the threshold.

Tina flinched. She wasn't used to being greeted as a married woman. But then, she'd been a wife for less than a year. Using all of the acting skills she could muster, Tina carefully smiled and stepped inside before she was denied access. "Hello, Sandeep. You look well." She was pleased that her tone was cool and friendly when she was a jumble of nerves inside.

The old man looked over his shoulder, as if he wanted to hide the signs that a lavish party was going on in her home. *"Sahib* didn't tell me you were returning tonight."

"He doesn't know." She removed the dark blue scarf from her head and let it fall around the collar of her shirt.

"Your hair!" Sandeep exclaimed, his eyes widening in horror. He winced at his unguarded words and abruptly bowed his head.

"Yes, I know," Tina said with a sigh. She wasn't offended. She had the same reaction every time she saw her reflection in the mirror. Tina self-consciously ruffled her fingers through the short tufts. Once she'd had ebony curls cascading down her back and had managed to get an endorsement deal for her crowning glory. Now her hair barely covered her ears. "It was a mistake."

Sandeep cautiously glanced up, his gaze returning to her chopped-off tresses. "And…how was your vacation?"

Tina stilled. Vacation? Was that what Dev was calling it? Did he think she was under his spell and incapable of staying away? The hurt scored through her like a jagged knife, so swift and ferocious that she couldn't move.

Her "vacation" had been more like prison. Like hell. The memory of endless white walls, the acrid smell of disinfectant and the oppressive sense of despair washed over her. She gritted her teeth and struggled to stay in the present. "I'm glad to be back."

The servant took a few shuffling backward steps. "I'll go find *Sahib.*"

"No need." Tina raised her hand to stop him. She had the element of surprise on her side and she wasn't going to waste it. It was time to act like the mistress of the house instead of an intruder. She only needed the role for a moment and then she'd gladly discard it permanently. "I know you're busy with the party. I'll go find him. Where was the last place you saw Dev?"

Sandeep gave a guilty start and looked at his bare feet. "It's hard to say." His mumbling words were barely audible over the dance music.

Was it in the arms of a woman or two? Tina's lips twisted with bitterness. Or was it even worse than she could imagine? She almost wanted a hint of what she would see, but she wasn't going to ask. This was Dev's home and the employees had been with him for years. He had everyone's loyalty and she was the interloper. "Don't worry, I'll find him."

The manservant's shoulders sagged in defeat. He peered outside the door. "I'll have someone take your things up to your room. Where is your luggage?"

"I didn't bring any." She didn't plan to stay long.

Sandeep frowned but didn't voice the questions that were obviously going through his head. He reached out his hand, his fingers lean from decades of work. "Shall I take your purse?"

She instinctively clenched her shoulder bag closer to her body. Tina forced herself to relax. "No, thank you," she said with a smile as she strode away. Sandeep wasn't the enemy, but she wasn't letting her passport or her money out of her sight. They were essential to regain her freedom. She had learned that the hard way when she had walked away from Dev while they were on a movie location in America. Today she wouldn't even let go of the rolled-up tabloid that was stuffed at the bottom of her bag. The one with her husband's picture on the cover. That photo and the accompanying story had lit a fire in her that still burned bright.

Tina walked to the center of the large entryway and stared at the sight before her. As she inhaled the stench of alcohol, sweat and cigarette smoke, she recognized a few of the guests. They were celebrities and actors whose faces graced billboards and movie posters. They still looked gorgeous, their damp hair and clothes plastered to their skin, as they moved feverishly to the heavy beat of the drums.

She narrowed her eyes and watched as two guests competed in a drinking game at the bar. So this was how her husband had spent his days while she was away. After reading the weeks-old tabloid, it shouldn't surprise her.

Tina wondered what the occasion was for the party. It had to be about business. The moment Dev was born he had been destined to reign this world. But it was not enough to take his rightful place at the top. He was driven to succeed, conquer new territories and gain incredible power. Money was secondary to this man yet every moment of Dev's day was consumed with business.

Well, almost every moment. She had been the exception. Once she thought that the aberration meant he loved her. Now she knew differently.

Tina continued to walk through the house. She wondered if he would claim that it was her welcome-back party. He was bold enough to try. And why not? He could lie and break promises without suffering the consequences. Dev was untouchable.

But her return had been impulsive. She hadn't known that she was coming back until yesterday. Now she wondered if that had been the wrong decision. Tina bit the inside of her lip as she walked farther away from the main entrance. Her goal was to show that she was no longer vulnerable. That she was stronger than her husband could imagine.

Tina hesitated before she moved deeper into the house. Once she had felt safe and comfortable here. She had even considered it her home. Now she knew it had been an illusion. Instead of being protected, she had ultimately been stripped of her power and freedom. Her fingers flexed nervously against her purse strap as she looked around, trying to remember where the closest exit was located.

She heard a group of people clapping and chanting loudly in the direction of the billiards room. Tina pivoted and marched to the back of the house, certain that her husband would be there. With his stunning looks, raw masculinity and star power, Dev was always the center of attention.

Tina rolled her eyes when she recognized the song the men were chanting. It had been from Dev's first hit movie. She had seen it countless times but she knew her husband was privately critical of his performance in it. He wouldn't play the song unless it was a special request for someone important.

She suddenly remembered the scene also included an actress. Would he be dancing with a partner? A certain ingenue? Bile burned in her stomach at the thought, but

Tina kept moving. She needed to see this herself and not rely on other sources. She needed to know.

Tina entered the billiards room unnoticed. She was invisible in this brand-name crowd. Her crumpled tunic and baggy jeans didn't cause one head to turn. The only time the Hindi film elite noticed her was when she was on the arm of her husband.

Everyone was facing the center of the room, jumping up and down with their arms outstretched as they sang. She stumbled to a halt when she heard Dev's bold laughter. The sound pierced her heart.

He sounded…carefree. Happy. Tina staggered back as the realization hit her like a fierce blow. How could he be like this after everything that had happened? Didn't he feel anything? Or was it just a relief to him?

Tina hunched her shoulders. Perhaps it was a bad idea to return for one final confrontation. She had always suspected that she had been a burden to Dev. She'd thought they had been desperately in love, but now she realized he had felt obligated to marry her. It hadn't helped that his parents had disapproved of the match. Of her.

Who could blame them? She was not worthy of him. His parents were Bollywood legends and she was from the slums. Dev had given up his parents' grand plans and eventually he'd given up on her.

Everyone had known it was bound to happen, believing she'd tricked him into marriage. They confused her with the bad-girl roles she had in those low-budget *masala* films. Perhaps Dev did, too. It had soon become obvious that she wasn't the brazen and sexy woman of his dreams. Dev had been ready to return to his playboy ways and he wasn't going to let a wife stop him.

And she wasn't going to let him have any more power over her. Determined to get this over with, Tina took a shaky breath and plunged into the crowd. She stopped, her heart lurching when she saw Dev standing alone in the center of the circle. He held the guests captive as he performed the intricate dance step with effortless grace.

Tina's chest squeezed tight. Dev Arjun. Her first love. Her biggest mistake.

She stared breathlessly at her husband, unable to look away. Dev was lean and muscular thanks to years of training for his popular action-adventure movies. Tina shivered as she remembered how his strong and athletic build felt under her fingertips. His golden skin had been warm and rough and she had enjoyed watching his rock-hard abdomen clench as she'd teased him.

She flushed, her skin tingling, as she watched Dev finish the iconic dance, encouraging the others to follow along. Yet no one could match his confident swagger or his bold and precise moves.

As he raised his hands up like a conquering hero, Dev appeared taller than she remembered. Larger than life. Tina noticed how his dark shirt couldn't hide his broad chest and how his jeans encased his powerful thighs.

She wished she wasn't aware of how good he looked, but this was a man in the prime of his life. His strength and vitality came off him in waves. In the past she had yearned to have those powerful arms encircle her. Now she knew to keep her distance.

As his audience roared with their approval, Tina dragged her gaze to Dev's face. Only then did she notice the darker shadows and the deeper lines around his eyes. His angular features were harsh and mesmerizing. He looked older. Harder.

Dev bowed before he accepted a drink from one of his friends. He tilted his head back and her gaze locked with his. Dev froze. He held the glass midway as his eyes widened. Tina felt his shock quiver in the air.

"Tina?"

His husky question scraped at her taut nerves. She wanted to melt back into the protection of the crowd. She wanted to run. She wasn't ready for this. She wasn't ready for *him*. But it was too late.

The room went silent. She couldn't speak, couldn't move, as Dev tossed down his drink and pounced. He moved with a swiftness that stole her breath. Her throat tightened as her heart thumped against her ribs. She suddenly felt cold as her muscles locked violently.

Dev captured her in his arms and gathered her tightly against him. She was trapped. She inhaled his spicy scent and tears sprang in the corner of her eyes as their most intimate memories assailed her.

Tina had imagined how she would act when she was finally in the same room as Dev. This was not part of the plan. She was supposed to be aloof. Icy cold. Untouched. Just like he had been during the last days they were together. This was the moment when she would take back her power and make her demands.

Instead, she remained silent as he slid his large fingers through her short hair. She stared at him as he firmly tilted her head back. Her mouth trembled with anticipation. She knew he was going to claim her with a hard and possessive kiss.

No! Tina reared her head back. What was she thinking? She couldn't lower her guard. This man was dangerous. He had weakened her defenses when they first met. Had turned his back on her when she'd been at her most vulnerable.

Tina felt Dev's arms tense as his eyes flashed. Was that hurt or anger? Suddenly he swept her in his arms.

Tina cried out in alarm as she grabbed the front of his shirt. She felt helpless and off-balance. Too close. "What are you doing?"

"Don't worry, *jaan*," he said as his crooked smile softened his harsh features. "I got you."

That was the problem! "Put me down," she ordered as she tried to get out of his hold. Dev's arms tightened around her. She was very aware of his heat and his strength.

"Not yet." She saw the gleam in his dark brown eyes as his smile grew wider. He carried her past the cheering crowd and through the door that led to the enclosed courtyard.

She craned her neck, looking around the lush garden. The fountain sprayed cold water and garlands of tiny white lights were draped on the thick bushes and trees. She heard Dev's footsteps on the stone walkway but she didn't see anyone else around.

"Put me down," she said firmly. "I don't know what you're up to, but that display was unnecessary."

Dev tilted his head. "Display? I was welcoming my wife home."

He couldn't be serious! She glanced at the top floor of their home where the bedroom was located. Panic coursed through her veins as the dark excitement curled around her chest. She was ashamed of her body's response. How could she feel this way about Dev? After all he had done to her? It was as if she was conditioned to accept his touch with unbridled enthusiasm.

"Please put me down." She had to stop this before she did something she'd regret. Tina turned and kicked out. Her movements grew wild until Dev halted and carefully set her down. She looked away as her curves grazed his hard body until her feet touched the ground. Tina immediately took a step away.

His eyes narrowed as he watched her create more distance with another cautious step. "I didn't think I would see you again," Dev admitted.

"I know," she whispered. That had been her plan.

"Where have you been?" he asked rawly.

Oh, she wasn't revealing that. That would give him far too much ammunition. "Apparently I've been on vacation for months."

Dev frowned. "What could I say?" He raked his hand through his short black hair. "I didn't know where you were or if you were coming back."

If? "I walked out. I left you. I don't know how I could have made it clearer."

He placed his hands on his hips and glared at her. She knew her words were too abrupt. Too antagonistic, but it was necessary. This wasn't a ploy or a maneuver. She had walked out of her marriage.

"Where did you go?" he said in a low voice that belied his anger.

Tina jutted her chin out with defiance. "That's none of your concern."

"How can you say that?" Dev stared at her with a dark intensity that made her shiver. "You are *my wife*. I've been looking for you."

That didn't make any sense. He had abandoned the marriage long before she'd had the courage to leave. "Why?"

"Why?" His voice cracked like a whip as the tension vibrated in the shadowy garden.

Her heart pounded in her ears but she wouldn't give him the satisfaction of seeing her nervous. Tina gave a careless shrug. "Yes, why? You got what you wanted all along. Or were you concerned that I would pop up at the most inconvenient moment?"

Dev's jaw clenched. "You have no idea what I want."

"You don't want a wife," Tina said as she held her purse tightly against her chest as if it were a shield.

Black fury darkened his eyes. "Tina—"

"And tonight," Tina said, "I'm going to grant you that wish."

CHAPTER TWO

TINA COULDN'T DRAG her gaze away from Dev. She saw the storm in his eyes but he didn't move. The air between them crackled. A tremor swept through Dev's body as he forcibly restrained his anger. "You're not thinking straight," he said hoarsely.

How many times had she heard him say that? "So you're going to do it for me? No thanks." He had tried to take over her life. And for a while he had succeeded. She had been too grief-stricken, in too much in pain, to care.

Dev closed his eyes. "I never should have taken you to Los Angeles."

"Why did you?" She refused to respond to the agony in his voice. Although she had felt too weak to travel, Dev had insisted she accompany him to the United States while he filmed several scenes for his blockbuster movie. She'd like to think Dev had been so in love with her that he couldn't imagine spending a night apart. Instead, she'd barely seen him. She had been alone and isolated. At times she'd felt like she was being punished for some unknown reason.

Dev slowly opened his eyes and glared at her. "You needed someone to look after you. You were not yourself after the miscarriage."

His gaze clashed with hers and Tina's skin went cold.

Miscarriage. He said the word with no problems but it had the power to send her into a tailspin. It still dragged her to those tense moments when the fear choked her. When she was alone, making wishes and prayers that went unanswered. When the doctors told her that she had lost her baby son.

"Not myself? How would you know?" she asked. "You weren't there. You made it very clear that you didn't want to be married anymore. That there was no longer a reason."

His breath hitched audibly in his throat. "Is that how you see it?"

Tina looked away. She didn't want to think about how Dev had no interest in her, especially after she'd lost the baby. Not now, not when the dark and confusing emotions were rolling through her. "You were the first to walk away. What else am I supposed to think?"

Dev sighed heavily and speared both hands through his hair. "I didn't walk away—you *pushed* me away. You wouldn't talk to me or look at me. You moved out of the bedroom and—"

Tina's head snapped back. "Excuse me for grieving!" she hissed. She wasn't going to allow Dev to treat her emotions as weakness. "We all can't shake it off and return to our normal life the day after the loss of our son."

"Don't." Dev took a step forward. "Hate me all you want, Tina, but don't you dare suggest that I wasn't grieving. I didn't have the luxury of hiding away from the world."

His words were like a punch to the chest. Tina flinched as she stared at him with wide eyes. "Luxury?" He made it sound as if she'd had a choice. As if she'd willingly surrendered to the grief that almost suffocated her.

Dev stared at her with a mesmerizing intensity. "You

seem healthier than you did four months ago." He looked deep into her eyes and gave a satisfied nod. "Stronger."

He had no idea, Tina realized. She could stride into the house as if she were a queen and confront her enemy with the daring of a warrior, but it was all an act. Four months ago she had been broken, but Dev's indifference had crushed her. She had tried to put the pieces back together but she didn't think she would feel whole or strong again.

"I know how to take care of myself. I've done it most of my life," Tina said. There had only been one time when she couldn't. After the miscarriage, she had wanted to lean on Dev until she got stronger. Instead, he had taken advantage of her weakness. "But I'm not here about that." She needed to get this over with so she could move on with her life.

"How do you feel now?"

Powerless. Heartbroken. Determined. "I'm ready for the next step of my life."

Dev didn't move but Tina sensed his stillness. His tension. It was as if he could predict what she was about to say.

Tina's heart started to race. It fluttered wildly against her rib cage and it hurt when she took a deep breath. "I want a divorce."

"No."

She blinked at his immediate reply. Unlike her husky words, his refusal was clear and unemotional. "What do you mean, *no?*"

"We are not getting a divorce," he announced as he took another step closer. There was a wintry cold glint in his eyes. "I will fight you every step of the way."

Tina stared at him as her confusion rolled in like dark clouds. That was not the answer she had expected. She had imagined this moment many, many times and assumed Dev would agree with a brisk, almost impatient manner. It was obvious he didn't want her anymore. Why continue this sham of a marriage?

"I'm offering something we both want," she whispered.

"I want an *explanation*. I want to know what was going through your head during those days we were in America. How do you think it made me feel walking into that hotel room and finding that the only thing waiting for me was that note?"

Tina frowned at his tone. Her brief letter had offended him. Angered him. He was lucky she had given him that much. She could have poured out her broken heart, but instead she'd simply stated that she wanted to be left alone.

"Where did you go?" he asked.

"Around. Anywhere quiet where I could think. Where you couldn't make decisions for me," she said. "I needed time to decide what I want to do next."

Dev tossed his hands up in the air as the frustration billowed from him. "You didn't have to leave to do that."

But she had. Dev had too much power. She didn't know why he'd bothered making decisions for her. At times she wondered if he had forgotten her existence. "You took over my life." Her voice trembled as she tried to keep her composure.

"I was taking care of you the best way I knew how," he said through clenched teeth.

"No, you were getting back to your old life with as little inconvenience as possible," she said. "I was no longer pregnant with your child and therefore, no longer necessary in your life."

Dev reached out and grasped her arms with his large hands. "If that's how I'd felt, I wouldn't have married you."

"You *had* to marry me. What would have happened to

your brand if you hadn't?" His family had meticulously created his brand image for years as the romantic hero. The value and power of his brand would have taken a big hit if he had abandoned his pregnant girlfriend. "So you married me to protect your career. The magazines did features about how you had settled into family life but they didn't know how eager you were to return to your bachelor days."

"That is not what happened." His fingers dug into her arms. Tina sensed he wanted to shake her.

"Really? I know what I saw when I arrived here this evening. You were having the time of your life. Tell me, how many parties have you had in the past four months?"

"I wasn't celebrating. It's part of the business. You know that."

She knew that Dev Arjun lived and breathed the mainstream Hindi film industry. It wasn't work or drudgery. He enjoyed every moment of it. Dev was more comfortable on the soundstage than in his home. And from what the gossip magazines suggested, he preferred the company of starlets over his wife. "How many women have there been?"

"I've been faithful." His eyes glittered. "Can you say the same?"

Her eyes widened with surprise. Dev thought she had found someone else? She had never considered it. She had spent the past months fighting for her life, struggling to get through the next day, the next moment. But Dev didn't know that.

Did he think she was capable of gallivanting through the world, hopping from one bed to the next? The idea made her stomach curl. The only man she had ever wanted didn't want her. The man she had fallen in love with had been in her imagination. A man who loved and adored her. A man who would lay down his life to protect his family.

That man no longer existed. She wasn't sure if he ever had. Sometimes she wondered if she fell in love with the fantasy that the Bollywood movie machine created.

Loving that Dev had given her strength but it had also been her blind spot. She had lowered her guard and had tried to lean on him when she had fallen apart. Only he hadn't been there when she'd needed him. He hadn't been there for her during their entire marriage.

She thrust out her chin. "All I'm willing to say is that I want a divorce."

His eyes narrowed as he noticed she didn't answer his question. "And my answer is still and will always be no."

"I'm going to get one," she insisted as she wrenched herself away from his hold. "But first I'm going to get my things and move out."

Tina turned on her heel and marched across the courtyard. She prayed he wouldn't follow. She didn't want to be alone with Dev in their bedroom. She would already be bombarded with too many intimate memories.

That was where Dev held the most power over her. One touch, one kiss and she was his. She squeezed her eyes shut as she tried to forget how wild she had been in their bed. He had always been in control as he guided her to a world of pleasure.

"Tina, wait," he called out to her. "We can't get a divorce...now."

Tina stopped. There was something about his sudden compromise that put her on full alert. She slowly turned around. "What are you talking about?"

He didn't meet her gaze. "I'm negotiating with a few investors. Our film company has taken a financial hit in the past few months."

Few months? It was more like a year, Tina decided. She knew Dev's parents had wanted him to marry Shreya Sen, the daughter of a beloved Bollywood family. Had that arranged marriage happened, Dev would have been the most powerful and influential person in the mainstream Hindi film industry. His legacy would have been guaranteed to last generations. But she had ruined all that.

Dev approached her. "The problem is that they think I'm a lot like the characters I play. A daredevil, reckless…"

"That's what happens when you demand to do your own stunts." She understood his need to take risks. Dev had to push himself to the limit. She knew better than to ask him to stop, even when it tore her up inside as she watched him cheat death.

"But they think being married has changed me. They think I'm more cautious." He shrugged. "If I have a stable family environment, I come across as a better investment."

She did not like where this was heading. "What does this have to do with me?"

"We need to stay married—"

"Forget it."

"—until I get the backing I need."

"I'm not doing it." Dev could find backing elsewhere. There were so many people who wanted to be part of his world and his projects. Why was this deal different?

"Think about it, Tina," he said softly as he stood in front of her. "This means a lot of money. A better divorce settlement for you."

She frowned. Why did Dev always throw money at her? It was as if he knew she was constantly worried about her finances. "I have a career of my own. I can support myself."

Dev raised his hands as if he was trying to calm her down. "You used to, but you've been away from the camera for six months."

"It doesn't matter. Mumbai makes almost a thousand movies a year. I'll find something." She sounded more confident than she felt. Her acting career had been struggling before she met Dev. Her savings were almost depleted and she needed a job as soon as possible.

"You can find a role—a good one, a career-changing one—with the right connections."

"No kidding." It was a well-known fact of the industry. She kept auditioning for roles while the children of Bollywood legends were offered starring roles without trying for them. It didn't matter if they couldn't act, dance or speak Hindi. It wasn't fair, but it was the business. Every Bollywood movie needed a big name.

"I can use my connections for you," Dev said. "If you stay in this marriage."

"No, thank you. I didn't use them while we were together and I'm not using them now." Every reporter had suggested she had married Dev for her career. Those accusations stung, but most of all, she didn't want Dev to think it was true.

"I can find a project for you that Arjun Entertainment is producing."

"So you can control my career the same way you tried to control me?" she shot back.

He gave her a thunderous look. "I can use those very connections against you, *jaan*."

Tina's mouth dropped. "What are you saying? That you will have me blacklisted?" she asked in a horrified whisper as the tears sprang in her eyes. "If I don't agree to this arrangement, you'll ruin my career?"

Dev didn't say anything.

"I need to work." Her mother and sisters relied on her salary. Directors knew she was reliable and hardworking, but none of that would matter if the Arjun family made their wishes known. "You can't do that!"

Her husband was unmoved by her pleas. "Act like a devoted wife for the next two months—until after our wedding anniversary—and I will grant you a divorce."

Dev regretted the moment those words came out of his mouth. He would never destroy the career Tina had spent most of her life building. The only time he had kept her from working was when her health had been at risk. Even then, it had been too late. They had already lost their baby boy. He would do anything to make her dreams come true, but he wasn't going to lose her like they lost their son. She should know that.

But Tina had decided he was the enemy. An obstacle she needed to overcome. Since they had married he had treated her like delicately spun glass. Had been careful not to upset his pregnant bride. Not that it had done any good. They'd still lost the baby and it had created more distance between them. It was time to change tactics.

"Why are you doing this to me?" she asked brokenly. Dev couldn't bear to see her like this, but it was nothing like the deadened look she had given him four months ago. That had scared him in a way that still gave him nightmares. "Is this because your career suffered when you married me? Is this some sort of payback?"

"I need a wife." He needed Tina. His life had always been focused sharply on his career until the moment he had seen Tina Sharma on the stage during a wedding. The woman danced like fire. Her movements were sensual and spellbinding. Fierce and elemental. It was as if she was dancing just for him. He knew he had to claim her.

Their whirlwind affair had showed no signs of slowing down. They were electrifying in bed. It still amazed him that Tina had been a virgin when they met. She knew how to make him hot and rock-hard faster than the most experienced seductress.

He'd always known that she loved him and had never questioned it until the fire inside her had snuffed out. Dev had thought maybe her love wasn't strong enough to last a lifetime. It had begun to fade and nothing he'd done had been able to stop it.

Her love couldn't have been that strong. Couldn't have been real. Perhaps it had been simply desire. Infatuation. Maybe she had been in love with the fantasy hero he had created onscreen.

When he'd seen her standing in the billiards room tonight, his first thought had been that his mind had been playing tricks. He had dreamed of Tina every night and his wishes had spilled into his waking moments. Yet this time her beautiful face was bare and her ebony hair stood up in spikes. Her wrinkled and loose clothes concealed her gentle curves. He hadn't been dreaming. She had finally returned. He'd thought this was a sign that she wanted to save their marriage. Instead she wanted to break the bond between them.

"I don't want to be your wife," Tina said.

Dev braced himself as those words pierced him. He was going to change her mind. All he needed was time and the fire that had slowly extinguished between them would burn hot and strong again. Only this time he wouldn't ignore the signs of trouble. "Play along for the next two months and I will not contest the divorce," he lied.

"Two months?" She shook her head. "That's too long."

It wasn't long *enough*. "Pretend to be a devoted, adoring wife. It shouldn't be a problem for you."

Her eyes narrowed. "What's that supposed to mean?"

He wondered now how much of the love she expressed had been genuine. If it had been real, how could he have lost it so quickly? "You're an actress. You can do it."

Tina cast him a suspicious look. "And what do you mean by devoted and adoring wife?"

"We act like a happily married couple." At this moment, he would accept the fake intimacy and forced smiles. Anything that he could build on. "There are people watching us all the time. Servants, the public, our colleagues. We can't give them any indication that we're going to get a divorce."

"Does this mean you're going to act like a devoted and adoring husband?"

He frowned. "Yes, of course." He didn't need to pretend. His conduct shouldn't be questioned. "We will share this house and a bed."

She held her hands up and took a step back. "I'm not agreeing to that."

Dev gritted his teeth. Where was the newlywed bride who had been so eager to start their married life? Where was the seductive woman who would find him at his desk in the middle of the night and drag him back to bed? "You are in no position to negotiate."

Tina bent her head and curled in her shoulders. She wrung her hands and whispered something to herself. Dev watched as she struggled to make a decision. She acted as if she was making an unpalatable deal with the devil.

She suddenly lifted her head and met his gaze. "I will stay here for two months," she said furiously. "I will act like a devoted wife if I have to, but I am not having sex with you."

"Wait until you get an offer before you reject it," he said coldly. There had been a time when she couldn't keep her hands off him. Did she hate him that much? Was this plan to regain her love impossible? "But we will need to sleep in the same bed."

"Then you'll need to sleep with one eye open," she said with false sweetness.

"Tina, nothing you say or do is going to scare me off." He leaned down until his mouth almost brushed her ear. "Or are you the one who's scared? Worried that you'll reach out for me in the middle of the night."

"No!" She jumped back as if she'd been burned. "That was before I learned that you were not the kind of husband I wanted."

And he had two months to prove to Tina that he was the only man she needed. "We need to return to our guests," he said as he reached for her hand.

She crossed her arms tightly. "I'm in no mood to party."

"I don't care." Dev continued to hold out his hand. She had finally come back into his life and he wanted her at his side. He wasn't going to give her any excuse to create more distance.

She threaded her tense fingers in her short hair and looked down at her jeans. "I need to change first."

"No." She would barricade herself into the room the first chance she got.

Tina's lips flattened into a stern line as she debated her next move. Dev was tempted to grab her hand and gather her close. Hold her tightly against him until their heartbeats were in unison and their movements were one.

"Dev?" A familiar lilting voice carried through the courtyard.

Dev swallowed back an oath when he heard Shreya Sen's voice. He watched as Tina jerked her head up. She took a step back and glared at him. "What is *she* doing here?"

"Careful, *jaan*." Dev grasped her hand. Her fingers were curled into a fist. "You are supposed to be my devoted wife."

"Devoted?" Tina exhaled sharply. "Oh, I'll give you devoted. I'll give you such a performance that you're going to wish you never made this deal."

CHAPTER THREE

"Dev, where are you?" The click of Shreya's high heels announced her arrival before the woman appeared on the stone path. "I said I would act as the hostess, but that didn't mean—oh, Tina!"

"Hello, Shreya," Tina replied as calmly as she could while the anger swelled against her chest. Hostess? This woman who everyone wanted Dev to marry—his parents, the industry, the movie fans—had been the hostess in her *home?* How often had this occurred?

Tina glanced at Dev for confirmation. An explanation. He didn't look at her, and why would he with the Bollywood goddess around? Her husband had welcomed Shreya with a smile but she couldn't read his expression. Would he really be that blatant? Would he have installed his first choice of a wife in their home?

"I didn't know you were back," Shreya said as she ran her manicured fingers along her long black hair.

Liar, Tina thought with a tight smile. Shreya would have heard that Tina had made an appearance at the party. The woman not only wanted to run interference at any possible reunion, but she also wanted it to be known just how close she had become with Dev for the past few months.

Tina didn't need to hear it from Shreya. She had learned quite a lot in the rolled-up tabloid that was crammed in the bottom of her purse. The cover story had been a mix of fact and speculation, but it was the snapshots around Mumbai that had been like a dagger to the heart. How long have these two been lovers? Dev said that he had been faithful, but Tina wasn't so sure. He shared a past with Shreya and she wondered if they had reunited once he'd got rid of his wife.

Tina glared at the other woman. Shreya Sen had been voted one of the most beautiful women in the world. Tina reluctantly admitted the glamorous actress was stunning. She managed to be sexy and elegant at the same time. Tonight she wore a short and strapless red dress that accentuated her golden skin and feminine curves.

Shreya's gaze swept over Tina's casual clothes and bare face. "Nice haircut," she murmured.

Tina's hands clenched into fists and she refused to touch the short tufts. Instead she flashed a brilliant smile and curled her hand around Dev's arm. It was painful being this close to him. Once she had clung to this man, believing he loved and cherished her. Now she knew he would break her heart without a second thought, that he was doing this for a business deal.

She trembled as she rested her fingers against his muscular arm. Tina gritted her teeth when he covered her hand with his. She knew it was part of the act but she felt trapped.

"Thank you," Tina said hoarsely to Shreya as her pulse kicked hard. "It's a very popular style in America."

She felt Dev's arm tense as he looked down at her. Their gaze held and Tina realized she had just revealed where she'd been for the past few months. She needed to guard her tongue before she confessed everything.

"What do you think of my new look?" Tina prompted Dev.

"I like it," he replied, his eyes darkening as he reached up and tweaked the spiky ends between his fingertips.

He hated it. Tina knew he would but that didn't stop her. It may have been the deciding factor for such a dramatic change. She had wanted a fresh start and was prepared to shed her old self. Cutting her hair had been symbolic of the new and improved Tina Sharma. She'd regretted it the moment she had walked out of the salon.

"America?" Shreya's loud voice jarred Tina out of her daze. "Is that where you've been? People have been treating it like it's a secret."

"I wanted some privacy while I recuperated." Tina said as she rested her head against Dev's shoulder. Her throat tightened as she remembered how easy it had been in the past to make this simple gesture. "I could stay in America and not be noticed."

"Oh, Tina." Shreya clucked her tongue and shook her head. "You didn't need to go that far away. I'm sure you could walk around Mumbai undetected."

Tina took a deep breath as the cutting words found their target, like a stiletto under the ribs. She didn't need the reminder that her career was almost dead and that it had never reached the same heights as the guests at the party. "I wasn't willing to take the chance."

"Shall we go back inside?" Shreya suggested and motioned for everyone to return to the party. She was obviously unwilling to relinquish her role as the hostess.

"Yes," Dev said before Tina could make any response. He held her hand tighter against his arm as he guided her along the path. She was tempted to break free but she refused to show any clues of her crumbling marriage in front of Shreya.

As Dev and Shreya talked about one of the guests, Tina let the words wash over her. She didn't want to return to the party. She wanted to curl up in her bed and block out the world. But she knew that wasn't going to help her situation. She had hidden away for too long and lost everything in the process.

When she stepped inside the billiards room, Tina wobbled as a wave of tiredness crashed through her. She pulled away from Dev and struggled to remain standing when she wanted to rush out of the room, the house, her old life and never return.

"Stay here and I'll get you something to drink," Dev told her.

Tina sighed with frustration as she watched her husband and Shreya get swallowed up in the crowd. She didn't want a drink and she certainly didn't want to see Shreya wrapping her arm around Dev's as if they were more than just friends. She was glad it wasn't Dev who initiated the contact, but she noticed he didn't shake off Shreya's touch.

"Tina Sharma!" someone squealed over the *bhangra* music. "Where have you been?"

Tina stiffly turned around and saw two women approach her. Dread twisted her stomach and she gritted her teeth. Prisha was a choreographer and Khushi was a famous playback singer. Khushi was in high demand and did all the singing for the most popular actresses, and when Prisha was attached to a movie, it guaranteed success. Both of these women had power and influence Tina could only dream of.

"It's been a long time," Tina said as they greeted each

other with air kisses. "You both look wonderful." Once again she wished she'd had the chance to change into a party dress. Then she wouldn't look like the outsider that she was.

"Thank you. By the way," Prisha said as she placed her hand on Tina's shoulder, "I didn't have a chance to give my condolences."

Tina froze as the sudden tears stung her eyes. *No, no, no!* The grief surrounded her suddenly and threatened to pull her down. She wasn't prepared for this.

"It was such a shame," Prisha said, her insincerity shining through her eyes as she moved closer. "I couldn't believe you had miscarried so late in your pregnancy."

"It was a painful time for both of us," Tina said brokenly. She wanted to get away but she couldn't move her feet. She needed to change the subject but fragmented images flickered through her mind.

"Did the doctors figure out what went wrong?" Khushi asked.

Tina closed her eyes. She knew she would have to deal with these questions, but she wasn't prepared to share those dark moments with anyone. "No," she croaked.

Prisha gave a sympathetic pat on her shoulder. "I'm sure next time you'll be more careful."

Tina gasped as the pain radiated through her. She jerked away and glared at Prisha, hating how the other woman's eyes glittered triumphantly. How did she know that the guilt and confusion swirled around her mind at night? That she continued to question what she could have done differently to save her baby?

"She's just offering advice," Khushi said as she held her hands up in surrender. "You'll need to get pregnant again soon if you want to stay married to Dev."

Get pregnant? No, never again. She'd made that de-

cision months ago and it broke her heart to think she
wouldn't be a mother. But she refused to take another
risk. She couldn't relive the fear and hopelessness. The
devastation. It was a matter of survival.

Tina swiped the tip of her tongue over her lips as she
struggled to maintain her composure. "What are you
trying to say?"

"What everyone else is," Khushi said with a sly smile
before she strolled away, arm in arm with Prisha. "That
the only reason Dev married you was because you were
carrying the Arjun heir."

Tina refused to watch the women leave. She stared
straight ahead, the party a blur, as the anger bubbled
up inside her. She had no comeback or argument. She
had nothing to defend herself with because the women
spoke the truth.

Tina remembered the moment she had told Dev she
was pregnant. She had been uncertain how he would respond. She'd known the baby was going to change the
course of his life but she hadn't expected the excitement
to leap in his eyes. His wide smile and fierce embrace
had told her everything she'd needed to know. His immediate marriage proposal was more than she could have
ever hoped.

He was a better actor than she gave him credit for.

But no one thought she had deserved the marriage proposal. Moviegoers were furious, believing the seductress
should never get the hero. Her colleagues didn't think a
girl from the slums was worthy of the Arjun name. There
was a hierarchy in the Hindi film industry and she had
broken the rules when she'd married Dev. Some reporters and bloggers had gone so far as to suggest she'd got
what she deserved when she miscarried.

She jumped, her memories scattering, when Dev

thrust a tall glass of mango juice in her hands. "You look pale," he said with a frown.

"It's from the jet lag." She didn't want him to know how fragile she felt. Couldn't, not unless she wanted him to step all over her for the next few months. "If I'd had a chance to put on some makeup and—"

"Tina!" She turned to see Dev's best friend stretch out his arms before he greeted her with a hug. "Where the hell have you been?"

"It's good to see you, too, Nikhil." And she meant it. Ordinarily, she would not have anything in common with a man like Nikhil Khanna. Born into a Bollywood dynasty, Nikhil was rich, educated and had a flair for writing screenplays. Her family had no connections and she had not finished school, yet they had quickly become friends.

"It's been too long." Nikhil held her gaze and she saw the serious glint in his eyes. "Your husband missed you."

Her stomach curled with fear. How much did Nikhil know? Did Dev confide in his friend? "And you didn't?" she asked lightly.

Nikhil gave a dramatic sigh. "You have no idea how much I missed you."

Dev brushed his friend's hand off her. "Watch it, Nikhil."

Tina glanced up at Dev. She hadn't heard her husband use that tone with Nikhil before. She was surprised at the possessiveness etched in Dev's harsh features. Tina gave a cautious look at Nikhil.

The other man didn't seem to mind as he rolled his eyes. "Now you can deal with Dev's bad temper and late-night rants against the world."

"Dev?" That didn't make sense. Her husband was known for his charisma and charm.

"Like I said, your husband missed you." Nikhil reached for her untouched drink and set it down on a nearby table. "Let's dance."

Dance? Horror snaked inside her. "No, no." She took a step away and bumped into Dev's solid body. "Not to-night."

"How can you say that?" Nikhil said over the upbeat music. "You were born to dance."

She had heard that many times throughout the years. Dancing had been her escape and her creative outlet. She was constantly aware of the music around her and had to express it through movement. Dev had once said that he thought she couldn't go through a day without dancing.

And then suddenly her body betrayed her. Failed her. Her senses had shut down. She couldn't move. Didn't feel the music inside her. It was as if her mind blocked it all out. She hadn't danced since the loss of her son.

"The only person she's going to dance with is me," Dev announced as he wrapped his arm around her waist. "But first she needs to greet a few of our guests."

Tina gave an apologetic glance to her friend as Dev dragged her away. Within minutes, her face was stiff from forcing a smile as she met with the guests. They all were part of the Hindi film industry but they were not her colleagues. Once they had been her inspiration as she watched their movies and read about them in the magazines. Now she wished she had never met them in real life. They were nothing like the heroes and hero-ines they played.

"Why are you friends with these people?" Tina asked as Dev escorted her to another room. She had fielded questions about her absence but no one had really missed her. They were more curious than concerned.

"Only a few of them are friends," Dev admitted, giving a nod of acknowledgment to an actor as they kept walking. "Most of our guests want something from me, and they wouldn't hesitate to stab me in the back the first chance they get."

"Then why invite them into your home?" she muttered.

"Our home, *jaan*," he gently corrected as his fingers tightened against her waist. "This time it's because we have completed filming."

She frowned. She should've known that Dev would have immediately returned to work as if nothing had happened between them. "What project?"

His grip tightened painfully. Was it her imagination or was there a hunted look in Dev's eyes?

"It was a modern retelling of Majnu and Laila," he said tersely.

She was surprised he had chosen to do a romantic movie, especially one that followed the classic Persian love story. A romance that was more tragic than Romeo and Juliet with a poor man falling in love with a rich girl. They were forbidden to see each other and Majnu was driven mad with love. Driven mad by Laila.

"You should have seen his performance, Tina." One of the inebriated guests interrupted, looping his arms around Dev's shoulders. "It was stunning. It's like nothing you've ever seen. The grief! The pain! You could see him descend into madness."

Madness. Her breath lodged in her throat as she stared at Dev. She jerked out of his hold as if his touch burned her. She knew all about grief and madness. She had been surrounded by it. At times she thought it had engulfed her.

"I'm serious, Tina," the guest said, unaware of the maelstrom of emotions whipping between them. "It was chilling."

"I'm sure it was." She forced the words out as her chest squeezed her lungs. It hurt to breathe. To stand tall when she wanted to fold into a heap. "I'm sorry," Tina said to their guest as she pressed her hand against her head. "But my jet lag is getting worse."

"You should lie down," Dev said. "I'll come with you."

Tina ignored his outstretched hand. She was tempted to wrap her arms tightly around her body to protect herself. She didn't want Dev to touch her or be close to her.

"No need. I'll just get some water. I'll be right back," she lied as she hurried away. "Stay here."

Early next morning Dev glanced up from skimming the newspaper when he heard the chime of Tina's bangles. *Finally.* She had escaped the party last night and he wondered if she was going to hide upstairs all day.

He set down the newspaper as he waited for her to arrive at the breakfast table. Dev grimaced when he heard her hesitant footsteps. Was she considering another escape plan? That was not part of the deal. He wanted— demanded—a devoted wife and he was going to have it even if it meant he had to hunt her down and drag her to the table.

Tina appeared barefoot at the doorway, wearing a pale pink *shalwar kameez*. The tunic and drawstring pants hid her curves. She looked incredibly innocent and feminine, nothing like the seductress roles she played in her movies. But Dev knew Tina was not one or the other. She was an irresistible mix of sweet and spice.

Dev immediately stood up and pulled out a seat for her. "I expected you to sleep all morning."

She gave a little bobble of her head. "I would have but the jet lag has a strange effect on my sleep."

"And on your sense of direction?" Dev asked as he

watched her pass the chair he held out for her. "I found you sleeping in one of the guest rooms."

She dipped her head and hurriedly sat down across the table from him. "I crashed in the first bed I found."

He didn't believe it. Tina was avoiding their marriage bed again. Avoiding him. "That was not our agreement." He had gone so far as to gather her in his arms last night, intent on carrying her back to their bed. He had expected her to kick and lash out. Instead she had snuggled against his chest and given a sigh that had almost brought him to his knees. He had known he wouldn't be able to sleep next to her, not with his willpower in shreds. Dev had reluctantly returned her to her bed, tucked the sheets around her and left her in peace.

Dev sat back down as Tina added vegetables and eggs to her plate. Her eyes lit up at a serving platter that was covered with a towel. "Are those *pooris?*" she said in a whisper.

"The cook made these in honor of your return," Dev said and saw a smile curve on her lips. It was the first time since she'd arrived that he'd seen her happy. It had been even longer since he'd seen her show excitement.

She grabbed for the hot fried bread. "It feels like I haven't had these in forever."

He watched as she reverently broke the *poori* with her fingers. She inhaled the fragrant steam before she scooped up the lightly spiced potatoes with it. She popped the morsel in her mouth and her face softened. Tina closed her eyes and groaned with pleasure.

The sound stabbed at his chest. Dev's body tightened as the desire heated his blood. It took effort for him to lean back in his chair and study his wife instead of reaching for the *pooris* and feeding her. She was a sensual woman who enjoyed her food. She loved to cook as much as she loved to eat. But this was different. He was watching a homecoming.

"You missed *pooris,*" he murmured.

Tina blushed and covered her mouth with her hand. "I missed spicy food. Indian food. Good food."

She missed that more than she had missed him. "Why didn't you make it yourself?"

Tina stilled. "It's better at home."

She wasn't telling him the truth. The woman who found it satisfying to cook, who found pleasure in cooking for her loved ones, hadn't prepared a meal in months. Yet, she hadn't starved. In fact, she had regained the weight she couldn't afford to lose.

But why hadn't she cooked? Or danced? When they had socialized with their guests at the party, he had noticed that her command of the English language had greatly improved. Where had she been all this time? What had she been doing? And with whom?

Tina bent her head as if the food on her plate required all of her concentration. "Why are you at home, Dev? Shouldn't you be at work?"

He glanced at his watch. He needed to go to the Arjun Studios and decided to take Tina with him. It may be too soon to reintroduce her to work, but what if she disappeared while he was away? There had been no hint, no discussion, when she had suddenly left him in Los Angeles. He couldn't shake the feeling that she would do it again.

She wouldn't, Dev decided. Her career was too important to her and dangling his connections was just the right bait to keep her near. "I will this morning and you will come with me." He raised his hand to stop her complaint. "You want my connections? This is the best way for directors and producers to get to know you. And we have special guests waiting for us there."

"Who?" She stopped chewing and glanced up at him. The pleasure fled from her face as resignation set in. "Your parents?"

She didn't know. Dev stared into her eyes and knew she wasn't pretending. How could she not have known? It had been international news months ago. Even if she were in America she would have seen the headlines.

"No," he said gruffly. "Your family will be there."

"My family—my *mother* is at Arjun Studios?" Tina bolted from her seat. "Why? When?"

Dev thought Tina would have been happy with the news. He hadn't expected this level of panic. He had only met her family a handful of times as Tina had made an effort to keep her family away. He hadn't thought much about it until now. "What's wrong?"

She paused and bit her lip. "How did they contact you? Do they know that I'm back?"

"I contacted them. In fact, I've been in touch with them since you were missing."

She winced. "Oh, you have no idea what you've done." Tina clapped her palms against her cheeks as she began to pace. "What did you tell them?"

"What I told everyone. That you were recuperating from your miscarriage. They had no idea where you were. Why couldn't you trust your mother with the truth?" What had she been hiding that was so horrible she couldn't even tell her family?

CHAPTER FOUR

TINA BRISTLED UNDER Dev's question. She saw the disappointment in his eyes. He had no right to judge. She hadn't been selfish or unkind. She needed to protect herself and she wasn't going to feel guilty about her decision.

"My mother would insist that I stay married," she explained as she crossed her arms.

Dev studied her. "So you disappeared?"

Tina felt a sharp twist in her chest. "I did what was best for me." She wasn't going to feel guilty. She had taken care of her family for as long as she could remember and this time she had to protect herself.

"By shutting everyone out," Dev said with bitterness. "It's what you do best. But I didn't think you had it in you to turn your back on your family."

Tina whipped her head around and glared at her husband. "I didn't! You don't know anything about my mother or my sisters." She had made sure of that. She didn't want Dev to see the family dynamics. He would notice how she was treated differently.

"I know your mother is confused and hurt by the silence she's received for four months."

Tina rubbed her hands over her face. The secrecy had been necessary. Her mother wouldn't have been sympathetic. Reema Sharma was not just her mother, she was also her manager. It was not the ideal situation. For a while Tina had recognized that her mother's advice was not based on what was best for Tina, but what was best to support the family.

"I've kept in contact," she muttered.

Dev scoffed at her. "Paying their bills through your accountant is not staying—"

"How do you know about that?" She never discussed her salary and expenditures with Dev and she had been grateful that he had never asked. He was very traditional in his thinking that he would financially support her.

"When you first disappeared, I thought you would have returned to your mother's house," Dev said as he rose from his chair.

Tina groaned and rubbed her forehead. She tried to imagine the rich and sophisticated Dev Arjun visiting her mother's home. She was certain the entire neighborhood would have been there to meet him. And knowing Reema, she had charged for tickets. "How much money did my family get out of you?"

"I was happy to help out," Dev said with a shrug.

"You shouldn't have done it. They are *my* responsibility," Tina said. She hated how much her mother obsessed over money. Tina had been constantly told how much she had cost her mother—the dreams, the security, the husband. She knew she had been a burden on her mother and nothing she did would make up for it.

Dev glanced at his wristwatch. "We should leave for the studios," he said. "I told your mother that we would be there at nine."

Tina recognized the vintage timepiece. She had given it to him early in their affair when she had discovered he appreciated those works of art. Tina looked away as she remembered how she had teased him about his inability to be punctual when he had a collection of high-end and technology-advanced watches.

"My mother is peculiar that way." Tina couldn't shake off the dread that made her sag her shoulders and drag her feet. "When she says she'll be somewhere at nine, she really means nine."

"Let's go meet them," Dev said.

An hour later Tina sat rigidly next to her husband in the back of the luxury car. As the driver turned on a busy street, Tina clenched her hands into fists and bent her head. It had taken longer than usual for her to get ready. She was nervous about her first visit to Arjun Film Studios. He had not invited her before and Tina had been reluctant to drop by unannounced. She had always suspected he kept her away because she didn't meet up to the Arjun high standards. She knew she had to look the part as the boss's wife. Dressed in a bright yellow designer dress, stiletto heels and dark sunglasses, she looked like a Bollywood star. The ensemble was her armor, hiding her tension and uncertainty.

She glanced again at Dev. He was dressed casually in jeans and a black dress shirt. He didn't have to try hard to look like a movie star. "You don't have to be part of the reunion," she muttered.

"Is there something I should know?" Dev asked as he scrolled through the messages on his phone. "Do you not get along with your family?"

"We're fine." The driver took a turn and Tina saw the sign for the Arjun Film Studios. She studied the large modern building. "*This* is your film studio?"

"It was built a couple of years ago to meet international standards," Dev said proudly as Tina stared at the green landscape that surrounded the white building. The entrance was a tower of glass windows. "We have soundstages, recording studios and dance rehearsal halls under one roof."

All the necessities to make a Bollywood hit, Tina thought dazedly as she continued to stare at the building. The music and dancing were required for every *masala* movie. Only when she worked on a movie, her dance rehearsals were done in crowded rooms or outside in the sweltering heat.

Tina noticed the buzz of activity when she walked in the lobby with Dev. Young men and women, dressed casually in a mix of tunic shirts and jeans, were rushing around. They carried papers, cell phones and small glass cups of tea. There was a sense of urgency and creativity in the atmosphere.

Tina spotted her mother sitting on the bright blue chair among the contemporary artwork depicting famous movie scenes. Tina was surprised that tears pricked her eyes when she saw Reema Sharma. Her mother's long black braid was streaked liberally with gray hair and red henna. Her white embroidered *dupatta* slipped over her shoulders and her dark blue *shalwar kameez* strained against her voluptuous curves.

"Amma!" Tina said in greeting as she stood in front of her mother. Inhaling the floral scent that she always associated with the older woman, Tina bowed down and touched her mother's foot with respect.

"I hate your hair," Reema said as she pulled a spiky tuft. "What were you thinking? No one is going to hire you when you look like a boy."

"She could never be confused for a boy," Dev drawled as he greeted her mother.

Tina rose to her full height and glanced at Dev. She felt a pull deep in her belly when she saw the gleam of desire in his eyes. She blushed and hurriedly looked away.

How could he look at her like that, when he had seen her at her very worst? No amount of makeup or gloss could erase those moments when her eyes had been dulled, her hair lank and her face colorless.

What was she thinking? She didn't want Dev to desire her anymore. To look at her with such intensity that her stomach would clutch with anticipation. She needed to keep her distance.

"Would you like a tour?" Dev asked.

"Yes!" Reema said enthusiastically.

"Where are Rani and Meera?" Tina asked as they walked. She was very aware of Dev beside her. Tina didn't like the way he towered over her. It made her feel small and delicate.

"I told your sisters that I needed to speak to you alone," Reema said as she straightened her *dupatta*. "It's a shame that they're missing this. Do you think we'll meet any stars?"

"They will be working," Tina said. She didn't point out that her sisters didn't care about the Hindi film industry. They had other interests and goals, something her starstruck mother couldn't understand.

"Yes, but we will be with the boss," Reema reminded her. She glanced at Dev and then back at Tina. "We can always talk later, when we're alone."

"I'm her husband," he reminded his mother-in-law. "You can say anything in front of me."

That didn't mean a lot to Reema Sharma. She wasn't impressed with Dev's good looks or his male charm. Tina couldn't remember the last time her mother had said anything complimentary about a man. Her mother didn't like, respect or trust men. Not since the day her husband had deserted her with three young daughters.

"Is everything all right?" Tina asked as they walked

through the crowded corridor. When her mother wanted to talk, it was usually about money. Reema was always worried about when Tina was going to get her next role and her next paycheck.

"You tell me." Her mother's voice rose. "Where have you been?"

Tina pressed her lips together. She knew she couldn't tell her mother. Couldn't tell anyone. She glanced at Dev and fear pulsed through her veins in response to his intent look. It was as if he was waiting for her to reveal her deepest, darkest secrets. "I was in California."

"Hollywood?" Reema's eyes lit up. "Did you meet anyone famous? Anyone in the movie business?"

"There was a television director," Tina said, remembering the anxious woman who chain-smoked and drank coffee constantly. "I had lunch with her several times."

"That's good!" her mother said as they walked past several offices. "Did she want to hire you?"

Tina shrugged. "There was some talk about it." She didn't think the director had been serious, which was fine for Tina. She couldn't imagine moving away from Mumbai. It was her home.

"That's it? One director?" Reema asked. "You were gone for so long."

She decided to stick with Dev's vague answer. "I was recuperating," Tina said, ignoring Dev's curious gaze.

"For four months?" Reema shook her head. "That's not recuperating. That's retiring."

"It doesn't matter," she promised with a firm smile. "I'm back."

"It matters," her mother insisted and began to tick off a list with her fingers. "You haven't worked for six months and no one is sending you scripts. Moviegoers have forgotten about you. Your fans turned against you once they decided you were the seductress who tricked Dev into marriage. And your endorsement deals are going to dry up the minute they see your hair."

"I'll find something." Tina tried to sound positive but she was beginning to wonder if she had underestimated the challenges that lay ahead. She couldn't show any concern, especially in front of Dev. If he knew how much she needed his Bollywood contacts, he could dangle the promise in front of her to make her behave for the next few months.

"Here is one of the makeup rooms," Dev said as he guided through an open door. "We have over twenty of them for the main actors."

Tina halted at the threshold while her mother investigated. She had never seen such a luxurious makeup room. It was colorful and cheerful, with red chairs and sofas, small tables and a day bed. This was where the actors went between breaks and it offered everything from a plasma television to a fully stocked refrigerator.

"Look, Tina!" Reema said as she stepped outside of the attached bathroom. "The sinks have hot *and* cold water."

Dev frowned. "What do your makeup rooms usually look like, Tina?"

Tina hesitated to tell her husband. She was a working actress, not a star like him. She wasn't offered these perks.

"Makeup rooms?" her mother said with a laugh. "She's lucky if she gets to share a makeup room with the junior artists and backup dancers. Can we see one of the soundstages?"

"Of course," Dev said as he guided them out. "We also have a gymnasium, lounge and executive dining room for the artists and senior technicians."

"Ooh!" Reema clasped her hands. "Tina, one of these days you'll have to take me into the dining room. I might see a Khan or a Kapoor."

"I don't think I will be allowed in," Tina said. She understood the hierarchy in the Hindi film industry. "They are for the main actors."

"You are married to an Arjun," Dev said. "You will not eat with the production staff in the cafeteria or canteen."

Tina flinched at Dev's tone. It made it sound as if her hasty marriage had been her greatest career achievement. Didn't he notice that she didn't beg to work with him or use his name? She knew a lot of people thought she had trapped him into marriage out of ambition, but she didn't want him to believe it. His opinion meant more than anyone's.

"You need to get back to work right away. I knew getting pregnant was going to ruin your career." Reema gave a huff of exasperation.

Tina squeezed her eyes shut. She remembered the argument she'd had with her mother when she announced she was pregnant. It had brought up some old secrets and fresh wounds. Tina had always known she wasn't the son her father had wished for, but she didn't know that her mother had seriously considered sending her to an orphanage when she was a child.

Her infant son had not been planned, but Tina never thought of it as an inconvenience. "I wanted the baby more than I wanted to be a Bollywood actress." Her voice shook with emotion.

"And what happened? You lost both." Reema tossed her hands up in the air in surrender.

Dev cupped his hand on Tina's shoulder. This time her instinct wasn't to shake him off. Her tense muscles began to relax under the comforting weight.

"You should have gone straight back to work. Dev did." Reema gestured at him with reluctant admiration. "He didn't miss a step. You, however, took a prolonged vacation."

"I insisted that she take some time off," Dev said.

Tina went very still. She wasn't prepared for Dev to take the blame. She didn't need his help. Not anymore.

Reema stopped in the middle of the busy corridor and her eyes widened with horror. "Why would you suggest that? Tina's acting roles were getting smaller and her responsibilities to our family were getting bigger."

"You remember what she was like after the miscarriage." Dev's voice grew colder. "She was grieving."

"She would have snapped out of it sooner if she hadn't taken an extended break from work. The gap between movies isn't going to be easy to overcome," Reema decided. "I knew she shouldn't have married."

Dev's eyebrow rose from that statement. "What do you mean?"

"The moment an actress marries, her career is over. It wasn't too long ago when an actress had to hide the fact that she was married."

"Amma, please," she whispered. She was used to these sweeping statements but she couldn't withstand another fresh wave of guilt. She knew all about how her mother had had to give up her Bollywood dreams because she had gotten pregnant and had to marry.

"You can't just take off work." She turned to Dev and explained. "I have a family to clothe and feed. We need to pay for her sister Rani to complete her education. And her sister Meera is getting married to an engineer with a good family. I don't need to tell you how important her dowry is."

"And you expect Tina to pay for all of this?"

Tina felt Dev's gaze on her and gave a nod. She was the oldest child and the duty to provide had been placed on her at a young age. Once she'd wished she could have gone to school with her sisters, but that had been a luxury she couldn't afford.

"Of course," Reema said. "I always knew Tina was our way of getting out of the slums. Considering all of the beauty pageants, talent shows and modeling assignments we went through, I had expected Tina to earn more by now. I admit she's not a great actress, but plenty of Bollywood stars get by on their looks."

"I will pay for her sister's wedding," Dev announced. "And her dowry."

Dev's words gave Tina a jolt and she stared at him. "What are you doing?" she whispered fiercely. "That's not necessary."

He ignored her as he spoke to her mother. "And if you need anything, anything at all, contact my assistant."

"Why would you do that?" Reema asked as she gave him an assessing look. "This is between Tina and me."

"I don't want Tina under any stress," he explained. "She's recuperating."

"Still?" Reema said in a squawk. She turned and looked at her daughter with disappointment. "Tina, I did not raise you to be so weak."

Tina didn't respond. She knew the hopelessness she had slipped into was not her fault, and yet, she wondered why she broke so easily. She knew how to fight and push through to get what she wanted. Nothing came easy for her. After the miscarriage, she had fought so hard to feel normal but it hadn't worked.

"Tina is not weak," Dev said in a growl. "She won't let me take care of her, but I will take care of this."

Reema pursed her lips as if she was weighing her options. "Thank you, Dev. It's the least you could do since you kept Tina from working. I hope you won't interfere with her career in the future."

"Amma, you and my sisters are a priority," she vowed. Her mother still wanted total control over her career and had been furious when Dev had taken over. But that was going to change. Tina needed to start the process of removing her mother as her manager and taking more responsibility in her career. "I can still take care of everyone."

"From the looks of it, you can't even take care of yourself." Reema sighed. "And you need to do something about your appearance—"

"And here's the soundstage," Dev said as they approached the open elephant door. Tina heard the crew talking over the buzz of electrical tools and the pounding of hammers. She stepped inside and her mouth dropped open. The soundstage was huge but she was even more impressed with the electrical catwalks and lighting grids. Everything was top-of-the-line.

"Tina," Reema said in a hushed whisper. "Do you feel that?"

Tina slowly nodded.

"Feel what?" Dev asked.

"The soundstage is air-conditioned." Reema sighed. "Tina, you need to work for an Arjun Entertainment production."

Never. She couldn't be financially dependent on Dev. He was already too controlling, too powerful. "So I can work in air-conditioning?" she mused.

"Don't forget the executive dining room," Reema said. "And if you're lucky, he might throw in a spot boy."

Tina rolled her eyes. "I don't need one." She didn't have a spot boy to hold an umbrella over her when it was raining or supply her with a steady stream of tea. She could take care of herself.

She glanced at Dev and tensed when she noticed his growing look of outrage. "Are you telling me that while you were pregnant, you didn't have a place to rest, an air-conditioned soundstage or an assistant to look after you?"

"Of course not, Dev." It was only then that she realized Dev had taken many of the perks he received for granted. "My name is not above the title in a movie."

"I will not tolerate this!" Dev said in a growl. "From now on, I will make sure you have all the amenities you need when you are working."

Reema smiled and linked her arm with his. "Now, Dev. This is something we can agree on. Let's talk."

An hour later, Dev sensed Tina leaning back in her seat as she surveyed the atrium of the Arjun Film Studios. She drank her rapidly cooling tea while he sat next to her, checking his emails. The atrium reminded him a lot of their courtyard and it seemed out of place in the modern studio building. It was cool and peaceful, especially now that Tina's mother had left once she realized she wasn't going to see any movie stars.

He knew Tina had been embarrassed when Reema had negotiated to have Dev's driver take her home. She had made a production of how she would take the bus, or splurge and get a rickshaw. Tina had tried to stop it, but neither woman understood that he wouldn't allow a female to travel alone. Tina would soon discover that her mother and sisters would have a full-time driver by the end of the day.

"Why are you playing the attentive brother-in-law all of a sudden?" Tina asked angrily. "What possessed you to offer to pay for my sister's wedding?"

"I will take care of her expenses." He didn't know why this was an issue. He was wealthy and could afford it. "You don't have to worry about it anymore."

Tina crossed her arms and looked away. "Why would you do that? And don't say it's because she's family because we know that's not going to be true in two months," Tina reminded him. "I don't want to be indebted to you."

The anger flared hot in his chest. "It's not like that." Why couldn't she accept his help? What would it take for Tina to trust him again?

The cooing of a baby echoed in the atrium. Dev's heart gave a vicious twist as he felt the color drain from his face. His gaze darted to Tina. The tension pulled at the corner of her mouth and she closed her eyes.

When was it going to stop hurting? Dev wondered. When would he stop bracing himself when he saw a baby on a TV commercial or when a stroller came near him like it was right now?

He saw Shanti, a famous Bollywood legend who had dominated the silver screen a decade ago, walk over to their table holding a bundle in her arms. The baby squealed as the chubby hands pumped with delight. Grief washed over him and he fought to breathe. He barely noticed the nanny following behind with a stroller, as his full attention was on the baby.

Normally he would have risen from his seat when a woman or an elder entered the room, but he couldn't move. He knew Shanti had privately struggled with infertility for years while she played the motherly roles. She'd had her first child a few months ago and she wanted to share her joy with the world.

Dev flinched when he felt Tina's hand on his. She gave his fingers a squeeze before she stood up and fixed a smile on her mouth.

"Shantiji!" Tina greeted the star as she rose from her seat. "Congratulations on your daughter. I'm so happy for you."

Tina was shielding him. Taking charge until he was prepared. He should be the strong one, but this time Tina was looking out for him. It humbled him.

Shanti's smile was radiant. "Thank you. I hope it's all right that I brought Anjali here today," she said as she watched Dev. "I have to go dub some of my dialogue but I couldn't bring myself to leave her alone."

"It's not a problem," he said gruffly as he forced himself to stand. His gaze collided with the baby's big brown eyes. Anjali frowned and stuffed her fingers in her mouth.

"She's beautiful," Tina murmured.

"Would you like to hold her?" Shanti asked.

He felt the wave of tension crash through Tina. It mirrored his own. He knew his wife wanted to decline but she couldn't find the words. Before he knew it, Shanti transferred Anjali into Tina's arms.

Dev's throat tightened as he saw Tina hold Anjali carefully in the crook of her arm. It shouldn't hurt this much to see his wife hold a baby. Watching Tina blink back the tears shouldn't make him feel weak and impotent.

Dev wrapped his arm around her waist as he inhaled the baby's scent. It was agony. He wanted Tina to lean on him but she stood ramrod-straight. Together they could get through this.

Anjali's mouth turned down. Dev had no doubt the baby felt their pain. Sensed the sadness they tried to hide. Suddenly the baby started to cry. The sound pierced through the quiet atrium.

Tina tried to soothe the girl but it only seemed to make the baby cry more. Her movements became more frantic.

Dev rubbed Tina's back, wishing he could stroke the tension from her body. If only he could make a joke or a lighthearted comment, but his mind was blank.

"I think she wants her mother," Tina decided as she handed the infant back to Shanti. The movie star held her baby close and murmured a few words as the baby cried. Shanti reached into the stroller and pulled out a toy rattle.

Dev stiffened as he dropped his hand from Tina's back. The brightly colored rattle was the same as the one he had bought in anticipation for their child. It had been the first toy of many.

The baby's cries faded and Dev thought his knees were going to buckle. Tina reached for Dev's hand and laced her fingers with his. She held on tight as she silently offered her support.

"I'm sorry about this," Shanti said as she waved the rattle to distract her daughter. "Anjali is usually content and happy."

Dev barely heard Tina's response. He fought hard to hold back the dark emotions that threatened to consume him. It felt like an eternity before Shanti carried her baby out of the atrium. His shoulders sagged once the door clanged shut and the infant's cries retreated.

"She shouldn't have made you hold the baby," Dev said in a low rasp as he gripped Tina's hand harder.

"It's all right." Tina's voice was soft as she returned to their table. "She wanted to share her happiness."

Dev shook his head. He couldn't forgive the other woman's thoughtlessness. "Her daughter was due the same time as our son. Shanti knew this. She knew about the miscarriage."

Tina didn't look at him. "Maybe she thought we were over it."

The words were like a punch in the chest. "Over it?" he said in a harsh whisper.

"Look at how our family acts about the miscarriage," Tina pointed out as she sat back down in her chair. "My sisters never offered their condolences or visited me in the hospital. Your parents don't speak about our son. It's as if he has been forgotten."

"I don't want to forget our son." Their son had never gotten a chance to be born but Dev would always love him.

"I'm not going to forget, either." Tina's hands fluttered against her eyes as she brushed away a wayward tear. "I want to honor him in some way."

"*We* will," Dev said hoarsely.

She gave a sharp nod and took a deep breath. Dev knew the signs. Tina didn't want to talk about it anymore. He was tempted to keep talking, consider ways they could honor their son, but he knew he wasn't feeling strong enough for the both of them.

"Until then," she said briskly, "I need to find some work."

Dev rubbed his hands over his face. He wanted to tell her that she didn't have to work, and that she didn't have to take the first role that was offered. But he knew whatever he said would be taken the wrong way.

Now he understood why Tina was driven to work. It wasn't ambition; it was duty. She had taken whatever was offered and made the best out of it. And she would accept any role, any assignment, despite the fact that she wasn't healthy enough to work. He had to keep that from happening since she wouldn't take care of herself.

"You should take your time and consider your options," he told Tina. "The pressure can be intense. I know what it's like. I'm the only child and have to continue the

Arjun dynasty. There was a great deal of pressure from my parents to perform to their expectations. If I had failed…" He shuddered at the thought of it.

"But you didn't," Tina argued. "You exceed expectations every time. Your parents have almost always been proud of you."

Almost. He caught the word. His parents had not been happy with his choice of wife and they didn't hide their opinion. No matter what she did or how she behaved, they disapproved of Tina.

"I'm surprised they weren't at your party," she muttered.

"You really don't know, do you?" he said in a whisper.

Tina stiffened and turned sharply to meet his gaze. "Know what?"

He wasn't sure if he should tell her. He may have decided he wasn't going to treat her like a fading flower, but he wasn't sure how Tina was going to handle the news. "My father died."

Tina's lips parted in shock. "How? When?"

"Four months ago."

She slowly shook her head as if she was trying to make sense of it. "Four…" Tina closed her eyes and swallowed hard. "When?"

"The week after you walked out."

CHAPTER FIVE

"DEV...I'M SO SORRY." She flattened her hand against her chest. Her heart was pounding from the news. She felt shaky and off-balance. "I didn't know."

"It made the international news."

She heard the disbelief in his tone. "I wasn't following the news at that time," Tina explained. She didn't want to tell him that she'd had no access to the television or computer. No magazines or newspapers. The lack of media had been surprisingly helpful.

"The commemorations lasted for weeks. There's going to be another one at an award ceremony soon."

He probably thought she was heartless because she hadn't rushed to his side. She hadn't been there in his time of need. Dev didn't rely on anyone but she knew he'd had a complicated relationship with his father. That would make the loss even harder to bear. "What happened?"

"He had a heart attack and died instantly," Dev said.

Tina closed her eyes as the guilt slammed into her. "How is your mother doing?"

"She's fine and back at work," he said. Tina noticed how he spoke in short, choppy sentences. It was clear he didn't want to talk about it. "She's in London doing a movie."

Tina stared at Dev with incomprehension. What was it with the Arjun family? They didn't grieve or stumble; they kept working. They were like machines.

Or was this how Dev had learned to grieve? She had judged him for returning to work right away. For not showing his grief like she did. She didn't consider that this was how he coped. Dev didn't weep or stay in bed for days. He lost himself in his work. "She couldn't possibly be fine. She was married to your father for over thirty years!"

"Despite the fact that my parents were one of Bollywood's legendary lovers on film, their marriage wasn't a love match. It was a business arrangement. They led separate lives and rarely stayed in the same house together."

"Still…" she protested weakly. Tina had sensed that Gauri and her husband, Vikram, were more of a partnership than a couple. They had worked together to build the Arjun brand instead of the Arjun family. And yet they had managed to stay together. In contrast, Tina had been deeply in love with Dev and their marriage had fallen apart within a year.

"They were indifferent to each other," Dev said. "My mother reacted to my father's death as if he had been a colleague instead of a husband."

Tina shook her head. Dev hadn't been allowed to grieve with his mother. He hadn't been able to turn to his wife in his hour of need. How did he manage to meet every challenge head-on without breaking? "Wait, this means that you're in charge of Arjun Entertainment."

Dev nodded and gave a quick glance at his watch. "And I'm very late for a meeting. I'll have the driver take you home."

"And this is why it's so important to get the investors," she said softly as she rose from her seat. "The industry isn't too sure about having a daredevil in charge of one of the largest media companies."

Dev cast a suspicious glance at her. "They will soon realize that they have no reason to be concerned."

"As long as you can show that you have a stable family life." The deal he had offered her suddenly made sense. "Kind of hard to do that with a missing wife. My sudden appearance has made things very easy for you."

Dev reached out and curled his finger under her chin. Her skin tingled as he guided her to look directly at him. Dev was close—too close—as he leaned forward. His gaze dipped to her mouth and her lips stung with awareness.

"Whatever you're planning," he said softly. His gaze was focused on her mouth. "Don't."

She pursed her lips. "I have no idea what you're talking about."

"Remember the agreement," he said as he dragged his thumb along the curve of her lip. "I want—I expect—a devoted wife."

Tina frowned. Did he think she had the power to hurt him? That was laughable.

Dev's harsh features darkened and he abruptly dropped his hand. "I have several meetings and I'm late. I will see you at home tonight. Be good."

Maybe she was reading the signs incorrectly, Tina thought as she watched him walk away. She could have sworn she had seen the longing in his eyes and felt the tremor in his hand. Dev didn't really want her as a wife, but he still desired her.

And after everything that had happened between them, Tina was ashamed that she still yearned for his touch. She hoped he would never figure that out. If that happened, she would be powerless against him.

* * *

"Dev? What are you doing here?"

Dev glanced up from his computer and saw Nikhil standing in the doorway to his office. He had just noticed that it was dark outside and the office suite was quiet. Everyone had gone home. "What are you talking about? This is my office now."

He glanced around. He had always associated his father with this room. It was ostentatious with the oversize glass desk and the expensive gold conference table. The garish movie posters were splotches of color on the white walls.

"Tina returned home," his friend reminded him as he stepped into the office. "You should be with her."

Dev gestured at his computer screen. "I have work to do." It was where he wanted to be. He was in charge. He knew what he was doing. This was the only place where he felt in control.

He was fighting back some very elemental feelings when he was with Tina. He couldn't stop staring at her, remembering how she tasted and how she felt in his arms. He wanted to drag her to their bed and claim her in the most basic way.

But Tina didn't want him. Didn't want him anywhere near her. He had failed her and their baby and she didn't want to be his wife anymore.

He felt his friend's gaze on him. "What?" Dev asked sharply.

Nikhil hesitated for a moment before he strode to the desk. "I don't know what happened between you and Tina."

Dev tensed. If Nikhil noticed the cracks in his marriage, then the problems were so strong that he couldn't hide it any longer. He was a fool to think he could salvage this marriage, but he wasn't going to give up. Not yet.

"Nothing happened." Dev gave a warning look but Nikhil ignored it.

"That's not true. You've lost a baby. Your father. And pretty soon you're going to lose a wife."

Dev slowly rose from his seat. Nikhil was his friend but he had crossed a line. "You have no right—"

Nikhil crossed his arms. "Where did you and Tina go for your honeymoon?"

Dev frowned from the sudden change of topic. "We didn't. I had to work on a movie." It didn't matter that they didn't take time off to go on a honeymoon. When they were together, their surroundings had faded into the background.

"And where were you when Tina miscarried?" Nikhil asked.

Dev closed his eyes as the guilt swelled inside him. Tina had been alone and she hadn't been able to reach him. She had tried to put on a brave face when he'd finally reached the hospital, but he had seen the tracks of tears on her cheeks and the despair in her eyes. "On the set."

"Of another movie," his friend added. "And where were you when Tina was recuperating?"

In another country. Dev slapped his hands on the desk and leaned forward. "She doesn't need me hovering over her. She's told me that."

"And you agreed? That's not like you, Dev."

It wasn't. Before they got married, he'd wanted to help her in every way he could. She had declined, obviously uncomfortable with his offers. Now he wondered if it had anything to do with him. Tina wasn't used to having someone there for her. Someone who wanted to give without expecting anything in return.

"Nikhil, I don't have time to argue about this. You may think that I'm ignoring Tina but I have been a good husband."

"Seriously?" his friend said with a chuckle. "Dev, you're a great actor. You're a good friend and from what I've seen, a dutiful son. But when it comes to being a husband, you are the worst."

Dev flinched. "That's not true. I give her everything she needs." His friend didn't understand that his home was a battlefield. Tina had pushed him away every time he'd tried to take care of her.

But he hadn't been enough for her. Dev looked down at his hands splayed on the glass desk. When he'd arrived at the hospital and found that Tina had miscarried, Dev had never felt so impotent, so afraid. He had watched Tina fall into a dark place where he had been unable to reach her. He could achieve anything when he set his mind to it, but he hadn't been able to help Tina or save their baby.

Dev bent his head as he remembered one doctor asking about the support system Tina received at home. Dev had assured the doctor that he had provided Tina with everything she needed: the best medical care, a safe environment and servants at her beck and call.

But *he* had not been there. He loved Tina and had been excited about the baby, but he had felt as if nothing more should be expected from him. He had already gone beyond expectations by proposing marriage.

Dev glanced up to see Nikhil watching him with a knowing look. "Don't you have somewhere else you need to be?" Dev asked.

Nikhil tilted his head. "Don't you, *yaar?*"

Tina sat at her makeup table that evening and took another look at her closet. It was filled with her clothes, shoes and accessories. Untouched, as if waiting for her. Just like the small crystal figurine of a dancer she loved so much. It still sat on her bedside table, catching the light.

It was like that throughout the house. Tina had expected Dev would have thrown out her stuff or at least boxed it. She'd thought he would get rid of any reminder of her.

She looked down and stared at the bottles and pots on the makeup table. She reached for her new tube of lotion and dabbed a little on her wrist before smoothing it on her skin. Why had he kept her possessions in the house? Was it to prevent the servants from talking or was it simply that he didn't notice them?

Or was it something much worse? All this time she thought Dev had been indifferent. Had she gotten it all wrong?

Tina jumped when Dev's hand snaked around her as he reached for the tube of lotion.

"Dev!" She glanced at her reflection in the mirror. Dev stood behind her with a stern expression as he read the label on the tube. Her gaze traveled from his hair, damp from a shower, to the dark emotions swirling in his eyes. His golden skin captured her attention. She watched as a few water droplets meandered down his bare chest. Her gaze continued to travel down. Tina shifted in her seat as she noticed the way his blue drawstring pants hung low on his lean hips.

"Please give that back," she said quietly as her cheeks became mottled with red. She couldn't remember what the label explained. She hoped it didn't give too much away.

"What is this for?"

Tina turned around and stood up. She took the lotion

from his hands and set it on her table, desperately controlling the urge to hide it. "Does it matter?"

Dev placed his hands on his lean hips. "It might."

His words set her on full alert and she gave him a cautious look from underneath her lashes. Was he fishing for information or did he know more than she realized? "The less you know about a woman's beauty routine, the better."

He snatched her hand and turned it over before she could protest. Pushing the sleeve of her white *shalwar kameez,* he exposed the slender welts that crisscrossed her wrist.

Tina curled her fingers into her palm but she couldn't hide the marks from Dev. She never wanted him to see the scars. They were a symbol, a reminder, of what she had been capable of when she was at her weakest.

"I noticed the marks last night when you were sleeping." He skimmed his fingertips along the ridges. "I never saw these because you hid them under your bangles."

His gentle touch made her shiver. She stared at his large fingers against her small wrists. Compared to his strength, she seemed fragile. Her marred skin only emphasized his perfection.

She tried to pull away but Dev wouldn't let her go. "I don't…cut anymore," she promised.

"When did you start?" he asked as he continued to caress her wrist. "And why did you do it in the first place?"

"When we were in Los Angeles," she admitted. She wasn't ready to explain why. She didn't quite understand it herself. All she knew was that she had wanted to release the pain that had been howling inside her.

"Why didn't you tell me?"

Because she had been ashamed. Horrified. And yet she hadn't been able to stop. She had felt compelled to hurt herself and watch the blood collect on her skin. "It looks bad now but I was recommended a cream that will make the scars fade."

She felt the sudden, angry tension in his touch. "I'm not worried about the scars," he said in a low hiss. "My concern is that you felt the need to hide this from me."

Tina yanked from his grasp. "I don't cut anymore," she repeated and she heard the defensiveness in her voice. "They are old scars and they didn't get infected."

"The next time you feel like doing this, you tell me," he ordered.

"There won't be a next time," she said as she walked away from him.

"How do you know?" he asked as he followed closely.

"Because I don't feel the need to do it," she explained as she entered the bedroom.

"That's not enough of an answer for me," Dev said. He cupped her shoulders with his large hands and turned her around so she had to face him. "Don't make promises you can't keep."

Tina ignored the way his hands seemed to leave an imprint through her thin tunic. She refused to acknowledge how close he stood. "Don't treat me as if I'm fragile. I can take care of myself and my family."

"You don't need to when I'm around," he announced.

"Is that why you came home so early?"

He gestured at the clock next to the bed. "It's almost midnight."

"I know." This was when the nightlife was starting and the ideal time for Dev as he tried to make deals and bring his colleagues to his club. "Everything okay at work?"

"I dropped out of my next movie," he said, unable to meet her eyes, "and I'm taking a leave of absence."

"*What?*" She snapped her jaw shut. "Why?"

He dropped his hands from her shoulders. "Because my devoted wife has returned home and I want to spend more time with my family."

"That may be your press release," she said as she marched to the side of her bed. "But what's the real reason?"

"You had complained that I was never there in our marriage. Now you're complaining that I'm taking time off to be with you?"

"I want to be left alone!" Tina grabbed her pillow and tossed it on the floor. "You became so overprotective after the miscarriage. I don't want to live like that anymore!"

Dev wasn't listening. "What are you doing?" he asked as he gestured at the floor.

She glanced at the white sheets and pillow on the floor. It wasn't going to be as comfortable as the oversized bed, but she wasn't going to get any rest if she slept next to Dev. "You made it clear that you wanted to sleep in the same room. I'm honoring my side of the bargain."

"What is that?" he asked as he approached her side of the bed.

"Haven't you seen this before? What am I saying?" she muttered. "You led a charmed life. This is a bed pallet."

"No, that is a couple of sheets and a pillow on the floor."

"In my family, it's called a bed," she explained patiently. "This is what I slept on all the time when I was a child."

He swiped up the pillow and threw it back next to his. "This was not our agreement."

She held up her hand to stop him from lecturing her. "You're worried about the servants knowing. They won't because it's so easy to pick this up and—*what is wrong with you?*" she shrieked as he lifted her in his arms and dumped her onto the mattress.

"You will go to great lengths to stay out of my bed." The anger vibrated in his low voice as he crawled onto the mattress and knelt between her sprawled legs. He planted his hands next to her shoulders before she could roll away. "Where was this reluctance when we met?"

She felt the blush crawl up from her chest and neck before it flooded her cheeks. "That was before I knew what kind of man you really are!" She should have known Dev would taunt her with her wanton behavior. Back then, she had been eager to discover a sensual paradise with Dev. She wished it was easier to resist him now, but she knew the pleasure she could find in his arms. It had been unlike anything she'd ever experienced and her body craved for his touch. Craved for him.

"Let me tell you what kind of man I am." Dev's voice was low and raspy as he leaned down until his face was right above hers. "I'm not known for my patience. I expect others to honor their word."

"And yet you can break your promise with no consequences?" Like the pledge he'd made almost a year ago to love her. Be there for her.

"I am also a man who hasn't slept with his wife for over four months."

Her muscles locked and her chest squeezed violently when she saw the hard glint of lust in his eyes. "I'm not having sex with you. We—"

"What are you so afraid of?" he asked.

Her stomach twisted with dark excitement. She knew not to push the issue about sleeping in the same bed and yet she had been reckless. She needed to appear cold and disinterested. This was a man who had never wanted to be her husband. What self-respecting woman would tumble back into bed with a man who had been indifferent to her during their marriage?

"I'm not afraid." Her voice sounded strangled in her tight throat.

"Liar. You're afraid that you'll submit to me. You're afraid it won't be long before you surrender. How little time it will take before I'm buried deep inside you." His voice cracked as lust deepened the lines in his face. "Do you want to find out, *jaan?*"

Tina stared at him as the blood rushed through her veins. He surrounded her and she felt as jittery as a wild bird ready to escape from her cage. Dev always had this effect on her. She hated the power he had over her but at the same time she wanted it.

Her hands itched to explore his bare chest and his masculine scent was distracting. Her *shalwar kameez* offered little protection from his body heat. It suddenly felt scratchy and confining. She wanted it off. She wanted Dev to remove it, slowly, reverently, as he kissed the skin he revealed.

Dev stared into her eyes and his mouth lifted in a crooked smile. "I already know the answer, Tina. Do you?"

CHAPTER SIX

TINA NERVOUSLY LICKED her mouth with the tip of her tongue. Dev watched the movement with an intensity that took her breath away. Stark need pulsed through her veins.

She didn't want to answer Dev. If she lied, he would prove her wrong. If she answered truthfully, he would demonstrate the accuracy of her guess. He needed to learn that she would pretend to be a devoted wife but he could not expect total submission.

But if she got out of bed, would he follow her? Her heart pounded wildly as she imagined his pursuit. She rocked her hips and the ache between her legs intensified. Tina bit her lip and Dev's eyes glittered with knowing.

He knew what she was resisting. He knew exactly how to touch her, how to please her. Dev would ruthlessly use that knowledge and she wouldn't put up much of a fight. He would strip her of her pride well before he stripped off her clothes.

"Yes," she said.

His harsh features sharpened, his skin pulled tight. His carnal look matched the primal need inside her. She sensed the tension coiling inside him as if he was going to pounce.

Tina suddenly realized that her reply sounded like a

request. A whispered plea. As if she wanted him to stay exactly where he was. She cleared her throat. "Yes, the answer is never."

He lowered his head as if he were in a trance.

"Did you hear me, Dev?" Her voice was edged with desperation. "It's not going to happen." She pushed at his shoulders ineffectively, careful not to slide her hand along the sprinkle of curls against his warm and muscular chest. "The only reason I'm in this bed is to fulfill an agreement."

He closed his eyes and she saw the fine tremor sweeping through his body. She felt his struggle before he opened his eyes. His gaze was dull and she wasn't quite sure if he saw her. He was focused on the battle within.

"I heard you," he said gruffly as he rolled onto his back and lay next to her. His movements were stiff and he sounded almost disappointed with her decision.

Tina quickly turned away from Dev and clutched onto the edge of the mattress. She bent her legs and curled into a protective position. She felt hot and her body throbbed for his touch. How was she going to resist him—resist every temptation—like this every night for the next two months?

She couldn't. She would have to play the waiting game. Once Dev fell asleep, she would slide out of bed and make a pallet. She'd remove all evidence that she slept on the floor before anyone woke up. Dev would never know.

The sag of the mattress was Tina's only warning before Dev curled up next to her, his arm lying heavy against her abdomen. Her legs jerked and she was primed to leap out of the bed. It took all of her self-control to remain still.

"What are you doing?" she asked as she felt his erection pressing against her.

"Not having sex."

"I made my choice, Dev." She tried to shove her elbow in his stomach, but he didn't budge. "I'm not about to change my mind."

"About the sex? I believe it," he said drowsily. "About staying in bed? You're going to creep out of it like a thief the minute I fall asleep."

"So you're going to hold on to me all night long?" Tina wasn't sure why she sounded surprised. Dev had always gathered her in his arms while they slept. Back then, the sweet gesture made her feel cherished. Now it felt like imprisonment.

His embrace tightened with warning. "Go to sleep."

"How can I?" she complained.

Dev's large hand slid along the curve of her hip. "I know one technique that always left you soft, warm and sleepy."

She shivered as she remembered how he would drag out the pleasure until her skin was bathed with sweat. Her muscles would be straining, her lungs ready to burst as her heart thumped wildly against her rib cage. She would beg, plead and threaten him if he didn't sink deep into her body. With each measured thrust, he had created a roaring fire that had consumed her.

"Cold?" he taunted, his mouth close to her ear. "Is that why you're wearing this old thing?" Dev pulled at her white cotton tunic.

"No." She had difficulty getting the word out of her mouth.

"Your negligees are still in the closet." Dev crushed the fabric in his fist.

"I know." She had avoided the lace and silk slips on

purpose. She had also tried to ignore another section of her closet. "So are my maternity clothes."

Dev's pause was almost tangible. He seemed momentarily at a loss. As if he hadn't expected her to mention the baby. Tina didn't move when his hand slid along her flat stomach. "I didn't want to get rid of those," he confessed. "Of anything."

Tina felt the tears well up. She blinked rapidly as her nose and throat stung. "Why not?" she whispered.

"Why would I?" He continued to stroke her stomach and the tender caress lulled her. "I knew you would be back."

"All of those clothes hold bad memories." It wasn't quite true. She had been so excited about the baby. Every milestone had been cause for celebration. She'd bought those maternity clothes in anticipation of her ever-changing body. She'd never had a chance to wear some of them.

"There were a few good memories," he said calmly as his hand moved higher. "I remember the silk nightgown you wore on our wedding night."

Tina shook her head. She knew he was trying to distract her from thinking about the unused maternity wear, but that nightgown represented her naïveté. She had carefully chosen the white silk, believing the night represented hope and eternal love.

"I'm never wearing that again," she vowed. "Tomorrow I'm stuffing it in the garbage."

His hand spanned her ribs, just under her breast. "You'll wear it if I ask you."

She scoffed. "In your dreams."

His mouth rested against her ear. "You're not wearing anything in my dreams."

Tina clenched her jaw. "Go to sleep, Dev."

"Good night, *jaan*." She felt him flex his tense fingers

before he reluctantly removed his hand. "Do you want me to keep the light on? Are you still having nightmares?"

"No," she admitted. Those bad dreams after her miscarriage had been so terrifying they had ripped her out of a deep sleep with a scream on her lips. She hated that Dev had witnessed her fears. "I haven't had one for a while."

"Good," he said with satisfaction as he reached for the lamp and turned off the lights. The room was plunged into darkness. "But if you do, don't hesitate to wake me up."

She frowned at his offer. "What good is that going to do?"

He rested his hand on her head. Her scalp tingled and she was very aware of how exposed she felt without her long hair. "I'll chase your demons away, Tina."

She wished that were true, but she'd learned the hard way that he wouldn't be there when she needed him.

Dev watched the sun rising as he held Tina in his arms. It had taken her hours before she had fallen asleep. When her tense muscles had gradually relaxed, it had felt like a hard-won victory.

Tina had always been a restless sleeper but it had never bothered him. It had felt like she was searching for him even in her sleep. Tonight she had reached for him, muttering something indecipherable and quieted down when her hand touched his skin.

Now she was curled up tight against his chest. This was the closest they'd been since they'd lost their son. A sigh shuddered through him. Tina had slowly drifted away and it had gotten worse in the last days before she disappeared.

She was stronger now. He missed her long hair, the way it would fan across the pillow, fall down like a veil when she was on top of him, and how he could wrap it around his hand and hold her still. But he didn't mourn the loss. He wanted to sigh with relief at the sparkle in her eyes and the color in her cheeks. He wanted to swing her in his arms every time she fought back.

It almost hurt holding her like this. It reminded him of how things used to be. Holding Tina, touching her, loving her, had been a privilege he had taken for granted. He missed this intimacy. He missed Tina.

Did she miss him? He didn't think so. The only reason she'd come back was to ask for a divorce. He was surprised she'd asked for it in person. He had expected to get a call from his lawyer as the days dragged on.

But he was going to fight this divorce. Remind her of how good it used to be and that it could be that way again. But first she had to trust him. Forgive him for failing her. He didn't think that was going to happen in the next two months.

Tina stood excitedly at the tiny stall on the corner of the dusty street. The honking horns and the overlapping conversations were the sounds of her childhood. The scent of spices in the air mingling with the odor of garbage was familiar.

She straightened the *dupatta* that covered her short hair and looked around the old neighborhood. The day was wet with humidity and everyone moved slowly. A bright-blue rickshaw kept together with duct tape seemed to shuffle past. The handbag vendor had patches of sweat on his white *kurta shalwar* while haggling with a group of young women in jewel-colored saris.

"I can't believe you chew *paan*." Dev shook his head with disgust as he settled his sunglasses on the bridge of his nose. He leaned against the colorfully painted street cart as small cars and motorcycles drove by. "What would your mother say?"

"That it has no nutritional value and it's going to ruin my teeth." Tina had heard that lecture many times. She glanced up at Dev. "That makes it taste even better."

His slanted smile made her pulse skip hard. She abruptly looked away and watched the *paan walla*'s red-stained hands. The man layered coconut and spices on a bright green betel leaf before he wrapped it into a tight bundle. "My mouth is watering," she confessed to Dev.

"Want to know what whets my appetite?"

She blushed at the heavy innuendo in his tone. "You should keep your voice down," Tina said in English, casting a quick look at the *walla*'s face. He didn't seem to recognize what she said or who she was. "It was named one of the most recognizable voices in Bollywood."

"I believe it was the sexiest voice in Bollywood," he replied in English.

"My mistake." He had also been named sexiest actor every year, which wasn't hard to believe. Dev Arjun was charming, athletic and possessed a sex appeal that wasn't manufactured. He was gorgeous without even trying.

She gave a quick glance at him. For the past two weeks, Dev had stopped shaving. The dark stubble didn't soften his chiseled jawline or diminish his masculine beauty. If anything, it gave a reckless edge to his dark looks. The indigo-blue *kurta shalwar* he wore skimmed his athletic body. She tried not to notice. Dev Arjun looked debonair in a tuxedo and sexy in jeans and a T-shirt, but Tina always thought her husband was stunning when he wore the long tunic and drawstring pants.

"I thought we were in this neighborhood because you wanted to get *chaat*," Dev said.

"I want that, too." For months she'd eaten only for

sustenance, for fuel. Nothing had tasted good and it had been a chore at every meal to spoon the food into her mouth. Yet it was different since she had returned to Mumbai. She noticed the toasted warmth of cumin or the bite of cayenne wafting in the air and needed to taste it. Experience it.

"Are you sure you don't want to go to a restaurant?" Dev said as he placed a protective arm on the small of her back as a barefoot child with spindly arms and legs ran past them. "There's a really good one on the other side of Mumbai."

Other side. She knew he really meant to say *the good side.* The glittery and elite world where he ruled. The exclusive neighborhoods that she still couldn't enter if she didn't have the Arjun name and clout behind her.

"Those restaurants are not authentic. They make appetizers and snacks that are inspired by *chaat,*" she declared with her nose in the air. "You have to get *chaat* from the streets. Tell me you've eaten something from these *wallas* at some point in your life."

He shook his head. "My family considered it unhygienic."

"That just adds to the taste," she teased him. "I can't believe you haven't been to a bazaar or eaten street food. You need to see more of Mumbai."

"I was born and raised here," he reminded her.

"Not *my* Mumbai." She flashed a smile of thanks to the *paan walla* as she accepted the stuffed beetle leaf that lay on a small square of tin foil. As Dev paid with rupees, Tina tucked the treat in her mouth, resting it between her teeth and the inside of her cheek. She tilted her head back and moaned. "Ah, now that tastes like home."

Dev looked away abruptly. As if he couldn't stand the sight of her. Her stomach twisted and suddenly she wanted to spit out the *paan*. "Are you sure you don't want to get one of your own?" she asked.

"I'm sure." His words were clipped with anger. "Let's go find some *chaat*."

Tina hated his mercurial mood. He had never acted like that before and yet it was happening constantly in the past two weeks. Just when she thought they had found a truce, it slipped away. It was like dark storm clouds rolling in suddenly and blocking out the sun.

She also noticed that he hadn't touched her in two weeks. The briefest touch and flirty banter teased her, had her waiting for his next move, but nothing happened. He didn't hold her through the night or swoop in for a kiss.

She was glad about that. Just thrilled. Tina always knew that this day would come, when he no longer found her attractive. It was bound to happen. She may not have a hold on his senses, but he would never know how weak she was for him.

"*Aloo tikki* sounds good, doesn't it?" she asked with determined brightness. "I've always had a weakness for potatoes. Ooh, no. Forget that. What about *panipuri?*" Her hands fluttered in front of her mouth as she thought about the crispy treat that was filled with spicy water. "I haven't had that for ages."

"You could have had that months ago if you had returned home with me."

Tina decided to ignore that comment. "We should move faster before someone recognizes us. And unless you want to start a mob, stop giving money to the beggars."

"I don't know what you're talking about." Dev's attention was straight ahead as they navigated the busy sidewalk.

"You keep slipping rupees to anyone who asks," she said. "They're going to follow and ask for more. And the other beggars will see that you're a soft touch and it's going to get out of hand."

"It's okay, Tina. I can always get more. I just..." He snapped his mouth shut and gave a shrug. "I can't help it."

"I know." Dev didn't know what it was like to go hungry or worry about money, but she could tell how much it upset him to see the suffering. He had always refrained from asking her what it had been like to live in extreme poverty. Tina was grateful for that. She wanted to protect him from the ugly truth.

"Oh, look." She grabbed his arm and pointed at the magazine racks in front of a DVD store. "Movie magazines!"

"I know you love reading these rags, but you can't believe everything they say," he warned.

"I read these all the time when I was trying to break into the business." She turned the carousel until she found the weekly magazine she had always enjoyed. She gasped when she saw an old picture of herself on the cover. "Bollywood's Bad Girl?" she read the headline.

"That reminds me," Dev said as he watched her flip through the magazine to find the story, "how did your meetings go with your agent?"

She winced. "I don't want to talk about it." If there had been any good or promising news, Tina would have immediately shared the information with Dev. It was difficult to share the disappointing news with someone who had the Midas touch.

"It couldn't be that bad."

"Yes, it could." Tina paused and glanced up at Dev.

"The shampoo company dropped me from my endorsement deal because of my haircut."

He nodded as if he wasn't surprised. "I'm sure they had a clause about you changing your appearance without their permission."

"And I lost out on a role," she admitted as her shoulders slumped. "One of the Kapoors got it. I should have known. The director is a cousin."

Dev hesitated. "You know, Arjun Entertainment…"

She immediately straightened her shoulders back and continuing flipping through the magazine pages. "Thank you, Dev, but I can't work for you."

"But you can work for my competitors?"

His sharp tone compelled her to look up. Dev's frustration poured from him like billowing heat. "I hadn't thought of it that way."

"Actresses marry producers and media moguls all the time in Mumbai," Dev continued. "And when it happens, the actress only works for her husband's film company."

"Which is usually what the actress is hoping for all along. I didn't marry you for my career." He didn't understand. She couldn't—wouldn't—be financially dependent on him. He had displayed enough power over her life.

An emotion chased across Dev's face that Tina couldn't define. "Why—"

"Oh, here's the article!" she said, desperate to change the topic before another argument began. "*Huh.* Apparently, I have risen from the dead."

Dev scowled. "You don't want to read that. Nothing good comes from hearing the gossip about yourself."

"It says here that Bollywood's Bad Girl went wild in America. Drinking, drugs and dating countless men."

She made a face. "I'm surprised they didn't add an arrest record or a homemade sex video to the lies."

"That's not funny." His fierce expression sent a shiver down her spine.

She reached out and patted his arm. "According to this, one insider source thought you got the Bollywood mafia to whack me. There's something here about numerous sources suggesting that Shreya Sen was behind my disappearance." She frowned. "And how she got the last laugh because…"

Dev snatched the magazine from her hand. "These magazines are full of lies," he declared as he stuffed it back into the rack.

She stared at him. She wanted to grab the magazine and read the last paragraph again. There was no way that could be true. Dev wouldn't do that to her. Would he?

"Shreya Sen was the leading lady in your film?" She stumbled over the words as the anger and hurt shredded through her. "You are playing star-crossed lovers with the woman you were supposed to marry?"

"Calm down, Tina."

The fury built up inside her with ferocious speed. For one scary moment she thought that she was really on the brink of losing total control. "You know what, Dev? Forget our agreement," she said in a deceptively cool tone.

"Your career—"

"Is dead. Just like this marriage." The hurt swelled inside her like gaping wound. "But I might garner some interest with my dead career. Give that magazine a tell-all story."

Dev watched her cautiously, as if he was trying to determine her mood. "You wouldn't do that."

"I'll let them know just how the most popular action hero—the favorite romantic hero—tried to blacklist me in Bollywood. I can't wait to see how your investors will respond to that cover story!"

Dev's eyes held an unholy glow. "Be very careful, Tina. I'm about to call your bluff."

"This is no bluff." She took a step forward. "I've seen your worst and I survived it. You haven't seen what I'm capable of doing."

CHAPTER SEVEN

DEV WATCHED AS Tina stormed into the house and marched up the stairs. Her anger had not waned since they'd left the bazaar. Nothing he said on the way back home had seemed to pierce the cloud of fury that had surrounded her.

How could she think he preferred Shreya? Wasn't it obvious that Tina held him spellbound? It had been torment the past two weeks to refrain from touching her. Kissing her. He couldn't stop staring at her lips, remembering how they felt and tasted. He didn't want any other woman. He wanted his wife.

"Do you need anything, *Sahib?*" Sandeep asked as he closed the door.

Patience, Dev decided. Because he had officially run out of it.

He shook his head. "No, thank you, Sandeep. Any calls?" He hoped there was urgent business back at the office. Something that would require him to leave. Distract him.

Dev frowned. How often had he done that? Gone to work instead of confronting a problem head-on at home? Work came easily to him but relationships were a minefield he had yet to master. Maybe Nikhil was right. He wasn't a good husband.

"Yes, one message," Sandeep said. He glanced upstairs and lowered his voice. "Shreya Sen called."

Dev exhaled slowly. Even the old manservant knew how Tina felt about Shreya. Everyone had noticed but him. He should have picked up on the clues. He hadn't considered Shreya a threat to his marriage until now.

She had been a colleague and a family friend. She often called for advice. Two years ago his family had started discussions with hers about an arranged marriage. Dev hadn't been enthusiastic about the idea but the union made sense. And then he had met Tina.

The marriage talks had stalled and then broken down completely. His parents thought he was rebelling. Shreya had thought they both needed one last fling before they settled down. But he had found something with Tina that he hadn't thought existed. He had found love that didn't hinge on his box office success. He had a private life. A world that wasn't designed by publicity or the film industry.

He had allowed the fantasy of a family life to slip through his fingers. Now he had a chance to get it back and he was going to hold on tighter. Somehow he was going to get Tina to love him again. Only this time, the love would be stronger and wouldn't shatter at the first sign of trouble.

"Sahib?" Sandeep said. "Would you like for me to get Miss Sen on the phone?"

"No, that won't be necessary." Dev raked his fingers through his hair. "From now on, if Shreya calls, I'm not here."

Sandeep smiled with approval and bobbed his head side to side. "Yes, *Sahib.*"

Dev strode up the stairs and went straight to the bedroom. He was going to convince Tina once and for all that he hadn't slept with Shreya.

He paused when he looked around the bedroom. She wasn't there. He heard the scrape of the clothes hangers and immediately went to her walk-in closet. He followed the trail of her sandals that looked like they had been kicked off violently. Her *dupatta* was balled up in the corner.

He stood at the threshold, his heart stopping for one aching moment, when he saw Tina scooping up her clothes and throwing them into a suitcase. She was leaving. Again. She didn't believe him. Didn't trust him. Why did he think he could regain that trust?

"Don't you think you're overreacting?" Dev drawled as he held back the rising panic.

Tina didn't look at him. She didn't answer. She acted as if he wasn't there.

"I will not accept the silent treatment, *jaan*," he warned. He'd had enough of being shut out. "I'd rather have you shout at me and tell me what's on your mind than ignore me."

"Fine," she said. "When I got married to you, I was seen as the obstacle that kept you and Shreya apart. I was the villainess in the story. The seductress that stole you from everyone's favorite heroine," Tina said as she tossed a shoe in the suitcase. "While I was gone, you take the role of a man who goes mad because he can't have the woman he loves. That woman being Shreya." She threw the other shoe with more force. "You want me to ignore the gossip, but it's a little hard when everyone knows you handpicked Shreya to play Laila!"

"Those were creative and marketing decisions. It wasn't personal." People thought it was his finest performance as he played a man who was heartbroken and descending into madness because he couldn't be with the woman he loved. He hadn't been thinking about Shreya when he played the role. He had been thinking of Tina, who had spurned him and had disappeared from his life.

"Really? It wasn't personal." She walked to her makeup table and yanked open a drawer. She pulled out a rolled-up magazine and tossed it at him. He caught it by reflex. "Then how do you explain this?"

He unrolled the magazine. The headline read Dev and Shreya: Together at Last! and promised pictures of their rekindled romance. "Where did you get this?"

"In America. I had found an Indian grocery market and went in there to get snacks. I found that instead." She picked up the hairbrush from the table and threw it savagely into the suitcase. "Those pictures are not of two colleagues at work. That was in front of our home during the night."

"I did not have an affair with her. I have never had sex with Shreya and I have no interest in her. I was faithful to you." But the pictures were damning. He wasn't sure when they had been taken. Shreya had used one of the guest rooms on one occasion as they worked together on their roles. "You got this in America?"

She placed her hands on her hips. "Yes, why?"

"That's why you came home." Would she have returned if she'd thought he had been pining away for her? Would she have felt the need for one final confrontation if she hadn't seen this tabloid?

He threw the magazine on the floor and approached her. She took a step back and bumped against the wall. Dev grabbed her wrists and held her arms above her head. "Not because I was worried sick about you. Not because your family missed you. It's because of those lies!"

"I'm just supposed to believe you?" Tina thrust out

her chin as her eyes glittered with defiance. "Shreya wants you."

"No, she doesn't. Shreya is secretly dating a married director." Dev had to wonder if Shreya had encouraged the stories about a possible love affair to keep the reporters off the scent of the real story.

"You tried to hide the fact that she was your leading lady," Tina pointed out. "Anything else you're not telling me?"

"No," he said as he leaned into her. His muscles clenched as her soft body cradled him. "Shreya is no threat to this marriage. I have nothing to hide. I haven't done anything wrong."

"Nothing to hide? Then tell me, was Shreya your first pick as a wife?"

"Yes, but—"

"Then you met me and got me pregnant," she said harshly. "I put an end to those plans. Or at least a temporary hold."

And marrying her had been the best thing that had ever happened to him. "So you're going to walk now? Sabotage your future because you believe a tabloid story over your husband's words?"

"It took me by surprise." Her voice rose. "I'm not jealous or anything."

Dev hadn't seen her like this. She had dealt with overly familiar starlets at parties and zealous fans who wanted to sleep with him. His wife had always handled these situations with a sophisticated ease. Tina must know he was under her sensual spell. He didn't want anyone but her and he thought he had proved it every day.

"Fine, Dev. You win," she said in a growl. "I will stay for the remaining six weeks, but I have a few demands."

He slowly let go of her wrists and watched her intently.

What was she up to now? "You are in no position to make demands."

"When we are in public, you need to make it very clear that you are besotted with me." She glared at him. "Why are you smiling?"

"Am I?" He set his mouth in a firm line. Tina was staking her claim. He liked it. He liked knowing that she was protecting what she felt was hers. She hadn't done it that boldly before. Had he mistaken her silence for confidence instead of uncertainty? Did she think she didn't have a right to make a claim? That he would have rejected it?

"I'm serious, Dev." She crossed her arms and leaned forward. "You want to prove to your investors that you have a stable family life? Don't let them think you're having an extramarital affair."

Dev rubbed his hand over his chin, hiding the smile that wanted to break through. Tina was going to be so angry when she discovered that there were no investors. That he had foreign investor groups who were clamoring to work with him since they had discovered Bollywood made billions.

"Do you think I'm going to respond to threats?" he asked silkily.

She rested her head on the wall and sighed as if the fight was leaving her. "Can you at least act like I was your one and only choice for a wife?"

"Yeah, I can do that," he said in a husky whisper. He wished he had shown it earlier and more often. If he had, maybe he wouldn't have made Tina feel unwanted. "But I want something else in return."

She looked at him with suspicion. "What?"

"Tell me where you went after you left me in Los Angeles." He needed to know. He was sure he wasn't going to like the answer, but the not knowing was killing him. "And who replaced me during those months?"

Tina hesitated. She didn't have to tell him. She knew that Shreya wasn't a threat to her marriage. That she never had been. It seemed incredible that the ingenue would choose another man over Dev.

Tina wanted to keep her secret. She was afraid to tell her husband where she had been. It could be used as ammunition.

"Why are you so quick to assume that I was with another man?" she asked. His accusation bothered her. Did he think she was like the bad girls she played on screen?

"Why were you so quick to think I've been with Shreya all this time?" he countered.

Tina flattened her hand against her chest. "I'm not the one with the playboy reputation. I'm not the one who's been caught with photographic evidence. And I was a virgin when I met you."

She saw the possessive gleam in his eye and it made her skin flush. He loved the fact that he was her first and made no secret about it. But now the idea that he may not be her only lover had shaken him.

"You may have been a virgin, but you were not innocent." His gaze drifted to her mouth. He leaned forward and then stopped, catching himself before he kissed her. "You knew how to drive me wild that first time. And once you had a taste of pleasure, you were insatiable."

She blushed. "So what?" She couldn't let him know just how much his touch affected her. How she became almost obsessed with him and his body.

He clenched his jaw and a muscle bunched in his cheek. "There is no way you would have been celibate while we were apart," he decided. "You are too sensual and too passionate to have slept alone."

"That's your evidence? You are using the way I respond to you as proof that I can't be faithful? Where is the logic in that?" she asked angrily. She had given herself freely to him and he was using it against her.

Dev's eyes darkened. "How do I know you wouldn't respond like that to all your lovers?"

All? "Did you ever think that I'm only that way with you?" she said in a hiss. "That I don't feel that way about another man? Why would I take another lover to my bed when I could have you?"

His lips tilted into a slow, sexy smile. Dev's eyes glowed with interest as he flattened his hands on the wall above her head, caging her in. "Tell me more."

"Shut up." She shouldn't have revealed that. He was already arrogant and cocky. Now he knew just how much she wanted him. How much she had always wanted him.

"You walked out on me," Dev said and closed his eyes. "What better way to get back at me than to sleep with another man? Any man would do."

She had walked away because she loved a man who saw her as an obligation. She had felt betrayed and discarded. She had thought the man she trusted didn't care about her at all. Yet the idea of getting back at him by sleeping around had never occurred to her.

"I wasn't thinking of revenge. I was in survival mode."

Dev raised an eyebrow. "Are you telling me you weren't tempted at all?"

"I wasn't looking! And even if I was, there wasn't a great pool of candidates where I was staying."

"And where was that?"

Tina covered her face with her hands before she blurted out the truth. "At a treatment center. For the past four months I've been staying in a psychiatric facility for depression."

The beat of silence stretched until her nerves twanged. She didn't want to see Dev's expression. The judgment in his eyes. The triumph that he could use this against her.

"Why didn't you tell me?" he asked, his voice laced with anger. "Why did you feel the need to hide that?"

"Because I didn't know if you would help me or use the information against me."

"I had been trying to help you."

She wanted to believe that but he had taken some actions that she couldn't understand. She dragged her hands down her face and caught his gaze. "You made decisions about my career and my finances without discussing it with me. You sent me to doctors who wanted to drug me."

Dev dipped his head. "I was taking any advice I could get. I had been concerned about you and I wanted immediate results. Any time I tried to discuss a problem with you, you shut me out. It was as if you didn't know what was going on around you. When you disappeared, I was out of my mind with worry."

"I'm sorry I worried you. I admit that part of it was to punish you. Part of it was to get away." She had been angry and hurt, striking out the only way she could. "I'm sorry for everything. I'm sorry you had to marry me because of the baby. I'm sorry that my body couldn't protect our baby."

"It's not your fault," he said. "We don't know why it happened."

She scoffed and looked away. "I feel like I failed. That my body failed."

"No, Tina. I am the one who failed," he admitted. "I should have been there for you and the baby. I wasn't because I didn't...I focused on the wrong thing. I was too busy providing for you and creating an empire for my son."

"You had to work," she said. "I know how competitive this business is—"

"That is no excuse," he insisted. "And after the miscarriage, I overcompensated."

"There was nothing you could do to intervene," Tina said. "Nothing could have saved our son."

"I couldn't save the baby, but I could have saved you. You were so frail and lost. But you made it clear that it was too little, too late."

"I needed you," she insisted. "I just wanted you there. That's all you had to do." She still needed him. She was always going to have that shadow of fear, wondering if the depression would return. Wondering if she would have to go through hell like she had for the past four months. She had already made the decision that she wouldn't have children to avoid it happening again, but what if that wasn't enough?

Dev curled his finger under her chin and made her look at him. "Tina, you are not weak. You are a strong woman who struggled with depression. The struggle is part of who you are now, but the depression will never define you."

She wanted to believe that. She wanted to believe that Dev could look at her and not see the torment that had overwhelmed her. She didn't want Dev to remember how she had been at her worst.

Tina pulled her chin from his hold and bent her head. "I'm sorry I've been a burden. I know I'm not the wife you wanted. You should have someone who will improve your life and be a business asset."

"You are not a burden." He sounded surprised that

she would suggest it. "I know that if the roles had been reversed, you would have done the same."

She couldn't imagine Dev sick or struggling. He could conquer anything. He had the inner strength that helped him meet challenges head-on.

But she would have looked after him if needed. She would second-guess herself, but she would have done what was best for him. She also wouldn't have walked away from him unless it was the only way he could be happy.

He wasn't happy now and he wasn't going to be for the next six weeks. He was miserable and moody. She was, too. It was painful being next to Dev without touching him. Without connecting. "We should end this now."

"Enough," he said gruffly. "Stop talking or I will make you shut up."

"We can divorce quietly and—"

Dev bent his head and claimed her mouth with his. Her knees buckled as she clung onto his shoulders. His fierce kiss lit something deep inside her. A dangerous fire that she had tried so hard to ignore. It roared through her veins as she returned his kiss.

Tina whimpered when Dev pulled away. Her stomach clenched with anticipation when she saw the lust flaring in his eyes. She didn't protest when he lifted her up. Instead, she wrapped her legs around his waist and grabbed the back of his head. She kissed him hard as he carried her to the bed.

CHAPTER EIGHT

Tina tightened her hold on Dev as he laid her down on the bed. She didn't want to let go. She yearned for the feel of him under her hands. She skimmed her fingers down his strong back and bunched his tunic in her fist. She didn't want anything to stand in the way of her skin touching his.

She pulled his shirt off his head, barely taking a moment to break the hungry kiss. Clinging to his strong shoulders, Tina opened her mouth wide as she drew Dev's tongue deep inside.

Tina had missed this fierce touch. The ferocious longing. Her blood was pumping hard through her veins as Dev shoved her drawstring pants down her thighs. His large hand slipped under her tunic and he captured her breast.

Dev pushed aside her flimsy bra and she groaned with approval when he squeezed her breast hard. Her nipple tightened as it rasped against his rough hand. Tina arched her spine so she could thrust against his palm.

When he pinched her nipple, Tina began to rock her pelvis against his. Heat washed over her as a delicious ache centered in her core. She grabbed the hem of her tunic and tore it off over her head. Her bra followed.

Tina reached for Dev but he caught her wrists and

held them against the mattress beside her head. His hips pinned hers but she didn't feel trapped. The dark excitement pulsed through her body as Dev bent his head and took the tip of her breast in his mouth.

Tina tilted her head back and moaned as the fire crackled inside her. She curled her fingers into fists as the edge of his teeth scraped her nipple. Rocking her hips, Tina urged for more. She wanted it harder. Faster. She wanted it all and she wanted it right now.

When Dev let go of her wrists to cup her breasts, Tina reached for him and dug her fingers into his hair. She wanted to guide Dev but he already knew what she craved.

He drew his hands down her body, his touch untamed and possessive. He grabbed the hem of her panties and stripped them off. Dev drew back into a kneeling position and pushed her legs wider apart.

She stared at Dev as her raspy, choppy breaths filled the air. Her heart lurched when she caught his primal expression. For a moment she felt vulnerable as he rubbed his fingers along the folds of her sex. A wicked smile slashed through his harsh features when he discovered she was ready for him.

Dev's gaze clashed with hers. Slowly his eyes narrowed and she looked away. She wasn't sure what had displeased him. Did he see her uncertainty? Feel her hesitation? She parted her lips to say something—anything—just to break the tension that coiled around them. But Dev grabbed her hips and turned her over.

Tina gasped when she was suddenly on her hands and knees facing away from Dev. His fingers tightened against her hips as she felt his tip pressing against her. Dev entered her with one long thrust. Tina shuddered as her slick flesh held him tight, drawing him deeper, as she rocked against him.

Dev's guttural groan echoed in the room as he began a fast and furious rhythm. Tina matched him stroke for stroke, determined to capture the wildness that he sparked inside her. His hands were everywhere, caressing her breast, sliding along the curve of her spine, and dipping under her hips. His finger glided along her swollen folds as he drove into her.

The fire inside burned white-hot. Tina stiffened as the climax ripped through her. She cried out, her flesh clenching his. Dev clamped his hand on her hips with one final thrust, growling low when he found his release.

Tina's arms and legs threatened to collapse but Dev's hands held her up. Her body throbbed with pleasure as he withdrew and laid her down carefully. Tina slowly turned on her back, stunned and shaky, as Dev toppled next to her.

Tina lay sprawled on the bed and closed her eyes. The only sound she heard was her heart pounding in her ears, her rough gulps of air, and the quiet buzz of the ceiling fan.

What had she done? What was she thinking? One moment she was offering a quiet divorce and the next she was tearing her husband's clothes off. It had always been this way with them. The time away had done nothing to diminish the passion they shared.

It was more than passion for her. She didn't know if it was because Dev was her first lover and the only man she had loved. All she knew was that she wanted this skin-on-skin connection. She needed to be part of him. Even now she was tempted to turn toward Dev and curl into his body.

"This changes nothing," she murmured as the panic began to surface.

"It changes everything," Dev replied softly.

She clenched her jaw when she heard the low rumble of satisfaction in Dev's voice. "No, it doesn't. This was a one-off thing."

"I plan to make it an everyday thing," he said as he yawned and stretched. "Every hour. Every moment."

She tried to stop the shiver of anticipation. "It was just sex." For him. She needed to remember that.

He lazily stroked her wrist with the curl of his finger. "Mind-blowing, life-changing sex."

"It was a lapse of judgment," she argued.

The sound of his chuckle skated along her nerves. "It was the best decision we've made in a long time."

"There was no decision." That was what made it so humiliating. He kissed her and she went wild. It was like a spark that suddenly exploded. "It just happened."

"Because we held back until we couldn't," he said with disinterest as he laced his large, dark fingers with hers. "Why fight it anymore?"

"I didn't want this!" She winced at how her voice rose.

Dev's grip tightened and he slowly turned on his side. Tina wanted to leap out of the bed. He moved with lethal grace yet she didn't move a muscle. She knew danger was approaching but she was mesmerized by his hot, masculine scent. Tina bent her legs and crossed her arms against her breasts but she knew that wasn't enough protection.

"Are you saying I forced you?" he asked huskily.

She recognized the growing anger lurking in his voice. She had to be careful or he would prove once again just how easily she would surrender to him. "No," she said, refusing to look at him. "We just got swept up in the moment. I didn't mean to have sex with you."

"You had sex with me by accident?" Dev drawled. "How does one do that? Because it felt very purposeful to me. You knew exactly what you wanted and how. You were very specific—"

"You don't seem to get it," she interrupted as a blush scorched her skin. She blindly searched for the bed sheet and drew it over her. "We are ending this marriage in six weeks. I am not sleeping with a man when the relationship already has an expiration date."

"Yes, you are." He gave a fierce tug on the bedsheet, ripping it out of her clenched hands. "We are still married and we will live as husband and wife for the remaining six weeks."

She sharply turned her head and met his gaze. Her pulse skipped hard as she saw the determined glitter in his brown eyes. "And what if I get pregnant?"

He froze. Tina watched his skin pale as his mouth parted open in shock.

"We didn't use protection," she whispered.

Dev closed his eyes but not fast enough. Was that regret she had seen? Or fear? She couldn't tell but it didn't give her the comfort she desperately sought. "Tina—"

"This is a problem," she said in a hiss as the panic threatened to bubble and overflow. "I am never, ever getting pregnant again."

His jaw snapped shut. "When did you decide this? You loved being pregnant and you couldn't wait to meet our baby. You always wanted to be a mother. Remember how you wanted to have at least half a dozen?"

That was when she'd thought she was strong and healthy. When they first married, Tina had felt protected and invincible. Now she felt broken and weary. "I said that before I miscarried."

Dev reached for her. "Next time—"

She jerked into a sitting position. "There will be no next time! I'm not going to go through that again." Tina propped her forehead against the palm of her hand. "The loss, the pain…"

He sat up and cupped her shoulder with his large hand. "Just because you had a miscarriage, it doesn't mean it will happen every time you get pregnant."

But there were no guarantees. In fact, she was at a higher risk. She didn't feel like she would be whole again and another loss would break her completely. "I'm not willing to take that chance."

"If you're pregnant, I will give you all the support you need," Dev vowed. His voice was clear and confident. "This time I'll put everything on hold so I can be with you every step of the way."

"Be with me?" Her voice cracked. "How is that going to happen? We will be divorced by then."

His harsh features darkened as he frowned. "Do you think I'm going to walk away from my child?" Dev asked coldly. "Our deal is off if you're pregnant. If we have a baby, we are married forever."

He wouldn't grant her the divorce? *No, no, no!* She couldn't stay married to him. He would take over her life again. She couldn't let that happen. "No, that was never part of the agreement."

"Circumstances change," he said as he got out of bed. "It's our agreement now."

"I'm not staying with you, do you hear me?" Tina punched the mattress with her fist as the fear coiled tightly around her chest. "I can't be married to a man who tries to control every aspect of my life because he thinks I'm incapable."

"I thought you understood." He rubbed his hands over

his face and exhaled sharply. "I was trying to help you. And you can't accept that I went through hell, too."

"Hell? You want to talk about hell?"

Dev dropped his hands and she saw the pain etched into his face. Tina bit her lip and watched with fascination as he hooded his eyes. Had he kept it hidden from her all this time, or had she been so wrapped up in her own misery that she hadn't noticed?

"When I say that I will be there for you and that I will care for you," he said slowly, "it does not mean that I'm going to hold your hand and say all the right words. It means making tough decisions when you can't make them for yourself. It means doing what is best for you even if it gives you the right to hate me."

She went still. "What are you saying?"

"If you're pregnant, I will do everything in my power to keep you here." He placed his hands on his hips as he made his vow. "I will give you and the baby the best possible care. You will not work, leave this house or even leave this bed."

She drew her head back as she watched him with extreme caution. She misunderstood. She had to. "You would treat me like a prisoner?"

"I will keep you safe," he said gruffly.

"Wait a second. Do you think I somehow caused the miscarriage?" she asked huskily as her throat tightened with emotions. "I did everything the doctor prescribed. I didn't take any unnecessary risks."

"No, you are not to blame," he said. "I let you continue filming even though it meant long hours and hard physical work."

"You *let* me?" She hated how the tears stung her eyes.

"I didn't know that the soundstages you worked on were so unsafe. No pregnant woman—especially not my wife—should have been working in those conditions. I should have made you stop."

"You just told me earlier that I'm not to blame. Now you think my career harmed our baby."

He scowled. "I don't think that, but I'm not willing to take that risk. I will make sure you will not work in Bollywood while you're carrying my child."

"Don't threaten me!"

The anger crackled in the air as Dev strode to the bathroom. "These are not threats. I am outlining possible events. If you are carrying my child, this time I'm not letting you out of my sight," he said as he slammed the door behind him.

Dev was not going to get away with this, Tina decided days later as she searched for her cell phone in her handbag. She heard the screech of tires and the immediate cry of the car horns as her driver navigated the luxury sedan through traffic.

Tina punched in the numbers on her cell phone and settled back in her seat. Dev seemed to think he could get away with anything. He thought all he had to do was smile and he could get his way.

She noticed he'd changed tactics after they slept together. Instead of confrontation, he courted her. For the past week Dev had treated her as if she was a queen during the day and his courtesan at night. Tina shifted in her seat as she recalled how Dev had brought her to climax the night before. She wasn't armed for that kind of battle.

Dev answered on the first ring. "Miss me already, *jaan?*"

Tina pressed her lips together as her heart leaped from the sound of his voice. "Don't push your luck with me," she said sweetly in English as she glanced at the driver.

"I'm sorry I wasn't able to visit your mother," he said. "I had to go to the office for an important meeting."

She pressed the phone closer to her ear when she heard the shuffle of papers and the clink of glasses in the background. "You're still in the meeting? Why did you pick up?"

"Because you called. What can I do for you, Tina? Name it and it's yours."

Was he acting that way because he had an audience? Tina dismissed that idea. Dev liked buying gifts but it was nothing like the joy he received when he helped her. He liked turning a problem over in his mind and finding a solution for her. There were times when Tina thought she had embarrassed him with her gratitude. Those were the only moments when she had seen his shy smile and the red streak highlighting his cheekbones.

"I just came back from my mother's house where I heard all about the wedding preparations," Tina said. "You are being far too generous."

Dev scoffed at the idea. "Impossible."

"You're giving Meera and my mother everything they want!"

"Not everything. I can't give the bride the sports car she wanted to arrive in at the wedding. I tried, but there are none available."

Tina groaned. She didn't know about the car. Did he know they were planning to cover the car with garlands and roses? "You need to learn to say no. You have no problems doing that with me."

"Did I say no to you at all last night?" Dev's voice rumbled. "Or this morning?"

Tina tried to shut down the memory but she clearly recalled every angle and plane of his gloriously masculine body. Her mouth watered as she remembered how Dev's warm skin tasted when she pleasured him awake.

"Why are you doing this?" She dropped her tone and gave another glance at the front of the car. The driver didn't know English but she wasn't taking any chances. "We will be divorced before Meera has her wedding."

"It's the least I can do," he said seriously, the flirtatious tone disappearing in an instant. "I didn't give you the wedding you deserved."

She pulled the phone away and looked at it before she placed it against her ear again. "What are you talking about?"

"We eloped when I should have given you the wedding of your dreams."

"I liked our wedding." The words tumbled from her mouth. She didn't want to discuss that happy day with the man she was planning to divorce.

"You deserved more." The way he said those words made Tina's heart squeeze. "I see that now. I thought…"

"Thought what?" she prompted when his voice trailed off.

"That I had done my part by offering marriage," he said softly, regretfully. "That I had exceeded expectations."

"I know." Everyone thought he had gone beyond the call of duty and she should be grateful. "Why are you telling me this now?"

"I'm trying to make amends. I can't go back and fix that wedding."

"So you're going to make it up to me by giving my sister the wedding of her dreams? Taking care of it so I don't have to?"

"Something like that," he muttered.

"Dev, I liked our wedding. It was intimate and personal and most important, it wasn't a spectacle." She shuddered as she imagined what the wedding would have been like if they had invited the Bollywood royalty. "It could have easily been a circus, which was the last thing I wanted. I wanted it to be about us and that is what I got."

As the silence pulsed between them, Tina realized how much she had revealed. Her marriage, her growing family, was all that had mattered to her. Now she was on the brink of losing everything.

"I have to go," Tina said briskly. She was flustered and knew it came through in her voice. "I have a stylist and a makeup artist coming over to prepare for the award ceremony."

"I'll be home soon," Dev said.

"I made the mistake of telling my mother about the award ceremony," Tina said, wincing at how she continued to babble on when she should end the phone call. "She watches all of them and she's so excited. She thinks I need to make a good impression and wear a sari and hair extensions."

"Forget the hair extensions," Dev advised. "I'm beginning to like your short hair. You can't hide behind it. But a sari…"

She groaned at how his voice deepened with pleasure. Tina made a face. "I hate wearing saris. You know that. I feel clumsy and swaddled in those things."

"But you like it when I unwrap the sari and—"

Tina held her hand up as if she could stop him. "Enough!"

"Wear the sari."

His gravelly voice made her skin tingle. "Goodbye, Dev." She shut the phone off as the car pulled into her driveway.

She didn't know what to do with this flirtatious Dev.

He had been like that when they first met. He knew how to make her blush and how to coax a smile. And she remembered the gleam in his eyes when she flirted back. It had given her the courage to act a little bolder, knowing that it pleased him.

How could he tease her when the possibility of a baby was there? Tina's mood darkened and she looked blankly out the window. How could he find happiness when the cycle of loss and devastation threatened to continue?

But then, how could she have sex with him every night? Dev made sure they used protection every time but that wasn't the only thing she was worried about. The pull she had with Dev was getting stronger. How was she going to break that bond in five weeks if she kept making love with him?

An explosion of camera lights blinded Tina the moment Dev stepped out of the limousine and onto the red carpet. She heard the reporters yelling questions over the cheering crowd. Tina firmly held on to her smile as Dev reached out his hand. She grabbed on tight and stepped out of the car, praying her strapless pink evening gown stayed in place.

Dev released her hand and curved his arm around her waist as he waved to his fans. She wanted to curl into his body, rest her head against his tuxedo jacket and enjoy the possessive touch. She was proud to be at his side and for a moment, she felt he was just as proud to be with her.

"Dev! Dev!" A reporter with a microphone hurried to them. Tina had not been at an award ceremony before. She had never been nominated and she hadn't been famous enough for invitation until she married. Unfortunately, Dev rarely attended these events because he was always on location. But Tina knew enough about red-carpet etiquette after watching countless award shows on television. Since it was her husband's big night, she didn't wear anything that would detract attention from him. She also knew to step away and let him conduct the interviews. As the supportive wife, she wasn't there to share the spotlight.

She stepped out of his hold so he could do his job, but Dev had other ideas. He snagged her hand and laced his fingers with hers. He wasn't going to let her out of his sight.

"Are those the Arjun jewels?"

Tina turned to see a television reporter standing close. The woman thrust a microphone in her face as she stared at the yellow gold necklace that spanned past Tina's collarbone. The matching drop earrings were heavy and swayed with every move.

"Yes," Tina said as she pressed her fingertips on the necklace, revealing the ornate ring that went with the set. "Dev asked me to wear them tonight."

She had been stunned when Dev had presented the wide, flat jewelry box. She had heard about the Arjun jewels but never thought he would want her to wear them. Tina had been flustered and awkward when he helped her with the necklace. The gesture had almost felt like a sacred ritual. As if he was declaring to the whole world that she was his. His woman, his wife.

"And are you excited about tonight? This is your first award ceremony," the reporter said in a clipped, almost rushed tone. "You missed quite a few in the last few months."

Tina gritted her teeth. Now she understood why this woman had approached her instead of the big names. She was looking for a bigger story. An exclusive.

She wasn't going to get one. The media worked hard

to give the actors and actresses an image and then spent the rest of the time trying to tear it down. She was supposed to be beautiful and sexy, but chaste. Tina had broken that rule when she got pregnant before marrying Dev. She was supposed to be from the high echelons of society and hold on to Indian values. It didn't help that she was from the slums.

It was expected that she showed no cracks in her marriage even though reporters were eager to point out any tension. When she miscarried, she hadn't been able to show her distress or depression. Reality wasn't allowed to touch Bollywood stars. Her world had crumbled but she'd had to act as if everything was fine.

"You weren't even at your father-in-law's funeral," the reporter said.

"I look forward to the tribute for Dev's father," Tina said as she tightened her hold on Dev's hand. "He had an amazing career and influenced the film industry for decades."

"Were you close to your father-in-law?"

"Of course," Tina lied. Vikram Arjun hadn't wanted to have anything to do with her. Their relationship had been cold and distant. He'd offered no condolences or even acknowledgment when she had miscarried.

She would never reveal the truth. No one wanted to hear it and she didn't want to share how unwelcome she was in the Arjun family. The Bollywood fans watched the movies because they wanted to be swept away in the fantasy. They wanted the heroes, stories about star-crossed lovers, and the exotic and luxurious settings. Anything that didn't remind them of their reality.

She felt Dev tugging her hand and she excused herself from the ambush interview. Dev held on to her hand as they slowly made their way down the red carpet. Every reporter wanted to talk to her husband, who was up for several awards. Working the red carpet was nothing new for Dev while she just tried not to look out of place.

When they finally made it into the auditorium, Tina took a moment to look around. The enormous stage was big enough for an entire cast to perform dance numbers. The audience was filled with the most beautiful actors and actresses. As Dev guided her to the front row, there was a ripple of awareness. She heard the whispers and felt the stares but she ignored them. As they reached their seats, Tina saw her mother-in-law was already there.

Tina took a deep breath. It was going to take all of her acting abilities to remain cool and in control. She didn't falter when Dev approached the legendary actress.

Gauri Arjun didn't look like her son. Her delicate and feminine features were framed by waves of dark brown hair. The woman was petite and slender while her son was tall and muscular. Dev favored jeans yet his mother only wore traditional clothes. Expensive ones, Tina noted, to go with her designer shoes.

"*Maaji,*" she greeted in the manner Dev's mother had insisted on. She bent down to touch Gauri's feet. She felt clumsy as everyone in the auditorium watched her. "It's been too long."

"Yes, it has."

Tina knew she was probably being sensitive, but the woman could make any word or phrase sound like a reprimand. "I want to say how sorry I am for the loss of your husband. He—"

Gauri swept away her condolences with the wave of her hand. "Thank you. I see that you are wearing the Arjun jewels."

"She is an Arjun," Dev reminded his mother as he gestured for Tina to sit down next to his mother.

"Before you sit down, Dev, you need to find Rajinder," Gauri said, referring to a legend who only needed to go by one name. "He has to speak to you before the show starts."

Dev sighed and glanced at Tina. "I'll be fine," she said and gave a small bobble of her head. She knew that Gauri would either ignore her or unsheathe her claws the moment Dev left. It was nothing she hadn't dealt with before.

As she watched Dev walk away, Gauri immediately turned to Tina. "I feel the need to be honest," the older woman declared.

Tina's muscles locked as she braced herself. It was never good when someone warned they were going to be honest. She wanted to hunch her shoulders and bend her head. Instead she straightened her spine and thrust her chin out.

"You should not wear those jewels," Gauri said as she flicked her gaze over Tina's throat. "You don't have the pedigree or the right to wear them!"

Tina bit her tongue as she held her hands tightly in her lap. She wanted to answer back. Stand up for herself, but she didn't say anything. The Hindi film industry thought she wasn't worthy of her husband. Sometimes she sensed that her husband had felt that way, too.

"Everyone knows that Dev only married you because you were carrying the heir to the Arjun dynasty," Gauri said.

"You mean your grandchild," she murmured. She would have shielded her baby from the pressure of the Arjun legacy and the expectations of becoming the next

Bollywood megastar. She knew Dev would have felt the same way.

"We could have started grooming this baby for greatness," Gauri said and then gave a shrug, "as long as it inherited your looks and not your acting abilities."

Tina let the backhanded compliment slide. She knew she got most of her roles because of her appearance and dancing skills. Her achievements were small compared to the rest of the audience at this ceremony, but she'd worked hard and made a career.

"Now you're back and Dev has taken time off from work? He backed out on a movie that was a surefire hit?" The anger vibrated in Gauri's voice. "And at the worst time. I can't tolerate this any longer."

"I think this is a conversation you should have with your son," Tina murmured. She gave a sidelong glance and noticed other guests were trying to listen into their conversation.

"Nonsense. You tricked Dev into marrying you in order to help your career." The older woman's voice sharpened with impatience. "That didn't work out. You disappeared and now you have returned. I want to know what you want."

She wanted a fresh start. Before she returned to Mumbai, Tina had thought that meant a life without Dev. Now, she wasn't so sure. There were too many times that she imagined staying with Dev and creating a family.

"What do I want?" she asked as she watched Dev walking back to her. He was sophisticated and gorgeous. A true megastar. But her favorite memories were those quiet moments at home when they'd prepared for the birth of their child. "I want him to be happy."

Gauri rolled her eyes. "The only way that's going to

happen is if you leave him," she said decisively. "For good."

Tina's polite smile dipped. She was often in dis-agreement with Gauri Arjun, but this time she knew her mother-in-law was right.

CHAPTER NINE

TINA PACED THE courtyard, hoping to find serenity, but nothing relieved her agitation. Her high heels clicked against the stone path and the stack of bangles clattered with every move. The water fountains gurgled loudly and the fragrance of the flowers was overpowering. The morning sun was unbearable. She pulled at the neckline of her designer wrap dress. It felt tight and suffocating.

Why had she ever agreed to this?

"Tina?"

She whirled around at the sound of Dev's voice. Her pulse skipped hard when she saw him walking barefoot down the path. His hair was getting long and a hint of a beard darkened his jaw. Today he wore a long blue tunic and faded jeans but the casual wear didn't hide his powerful and masculine body.

She felt a flutter low in her belly when she saw the lust flare in his dark eyes. She was keenly aware of how the dress clung to her curves. Tina clasped her hands in front of her and remained still as her heart beat fast.

"Sandeep told me you had asked for the car. Where are you going? An audition?"

Tina went still and nervously licked her lips. "I'm going to a charity luncheon."

"Really?" His eyes narrowed on her mouth and he

strolled closer. "You should have told me. I had made plans for us today."

She gave a guilty start. "I'm sorry. I didn't know until the last minute."

He didn't say anything as he watched the blush stain her cheeks. "What charity is it?" he asked silkily.

She gritted her teeth. She was reluctant to share any information and she wasn't sure why. No, that wasn't true. She knew this was going to trigger a discussion she didn't want to have with Dev.

"Tina?" His voice held a steely edge.

She looked away. "It's for mothers who have suffered miscarriages."

The silence pulsed in the courtyard. She gave a cautious glance in Dev's direction. Dread settled in her chest as she watched Dev's harsh features sharpen. She saw the way he clenched his jaw and the hurt that flashed through his eyes.

"They want to promote the resources they offer to these women and they needed a celebrity to get media coverage," she babbled on. "I volunteered. I thought this would be a good way to honor our son."

"Why didn't you tell me?" he asked coldly. "Afraid that I would want to come along? Steal the spotlight?"

Tina's eyes widened with shock. "No, of course not. It's a women's charity. I didn't think you would be interested."

He flinched. "Right, because I don't know anything about miscarriages. It hasn't touched my life, my marriage or my heart." He turned abruptly and walked back to the house.

"I didn't say that," she called out as she hurried after him.

He didn't look back. "You don't have to. You're shutting

me out like you did when you miscarried. You had to suffer alone. Deal with it alone."

"It's just easier that way!" she declared.

Dev stopped and slowly turned around. "Easier?"

"No, that isn't true. It's not easier." Tina dipped her head and raked her hands through her hair. She was used to carrying the weight of others—her mother, her sisters—but this time she didn't have the strength. She needed to rely on someone else but no one was there to help. Dev's absence had felt like a dismissal. A betrayal. She didn't want to put herself in that position again.

But as she looked at the hurt and disappointment in Dev's eyes, she realized she was guilty of the same thing she had accused him of. How many times had he reached for her, searching for solace, only to be rejected? She didn't know. She had been too focused on her own pain. How often had she believed that her grief was stronger, more powerful, because she was the one who had carried the baby?

"It's my fault we didn't have a chance to grieve together." She knew now that Dev hadn't been indifferent. He mourned differently. Silently. "I wanted to handle it alone and I couldn't."

"You got the help you needed," he reminded her. "I know that was a difficult decision for you, but you did it. You don't need my help anymore."

"That's not true." Her voice wobbled and she swallowed hard. She needed his help and he needed hers. "I want you to come with me to the charity luncheon."

His sigh was low and deep. "Tina…"

She raised a shaky hand to stop him. "I thought I could do this on my own, but I can't. I've been walking in circles trying to gather up enough courage to face this luncheon."

"You won't fall apart, *jaan*," Dev said softly.

He was refusing her offer. Tina took a shallow breath as her chest ached with disappointment. She shouldn't be surprised. She hadn't been there for him in the beginning and she kept shutting him out.

"You're right. I won't," she said as she walked past him. "But one of these days, I hope we can honor our son together. Maybe it's the wrong charity for you. The wrong venue. The wrong time—"

He grabbed her arm and she lurched to a stop. Tina looked down at his large fingers encircling her wrist. She glanced up and stared at the shadows and deep lines in his face.

"I'm still angry that our son didn't get a chance. So damn angry," Dev admitted. "You may want to share how you feel with a crowd of strangers, but I'm not ready for the world to witness my pain."

Tina pressed her lips together and nodded. She hadn't considered that Dev was at a different stage of grief and loss. While she'd had months to focus on her bereavement, Dev had been struggling on his own.

"But I will go to this charity luncheon with you." His voice was gravelly. "Because you are the only person I want to grieve with. If this is how you want to mourn, I will be there for you."

Tina's lips trembled as her throat ached with emotions. She closed her eyes before the tears started to fall. "And I'll be there for you, Dev." She wrapped her arms around him and leaned her head on his shoulder. "No matter what. I promise."

Late one afternoon, Dev stood at the door of Tina's dance studio. He remained quiet, careful not to disturb Tina as she swayed to *bhangra* music. When he had returned from America without her, he hadn't entered this room. As the days had become weeks, he hadn't approached this wing of the house. He'd known it would be cold and empty. The plain room didn't hold her spirit or reflect her personality.

Her dancing, however, revealed everything about her.

How often had he watched her films late into the night? Dev leaned his head against the door frame. He had to admit, the story lines and dialogues were awful. The editing was usually sloppy and the special effects were antiquated. But when Tina arrived on the scene, he didn't notice anything else. Her presence was electrifying and when she danced, the light inside her shone bright.

He knew how she moved and how she expressed herself through dance. It was sensual. Elemental. She could show restraint in the traditional dance styles and energy in the modern steps. Tina conveyed emotion from the tilt of her head to the point of her toe. Most men didn't notice that. They were mesmerized by the shake of her hips and her mysterious smile.

And he could tell right now that something was off. She was upset. Uncertain. Her movements were sharper and a beat faster than the music.

She stepped out of the spin. Her balance wobbled before she planted both feet firmly on the wood floor. Tina stomped her bare foot and placed her hand on her forehead.

Dev lifted his head as he felt a kick of concern. The clumsy move wasn't like her. She was innately graceful and had done that spin countless times.

The music continued to play. He recognized it from one of her movies. It was her signature song. The lyrics were audacious, saying she was going to steal the groom from the bride. The choreography was just as suggestive.

He moved forward without thinking about it. As he slid his arm on her waist, Tina jumped and turned around. Before she could step away, Dev grasped her hand with his and cradled her close.

Tina glanced at the door and then turned her attention back at him. "How long have you been here? Were you watching me?"

"A few seconds," he admitted as they glided across the floor just like old times. Dancing had been just part of the job until he'd met Tina. He'd wanted to be near her, share the music and move as one. He'd found every opportunity to dance with her at clubs, parties and the random moments in the courtyard.

Tina bent her head. "I can't hit the moves like I used to," she confessed.

"You're putting too much pressure on yourself," Dev declared as his hand flattened against her spine. As his fingers stroked the sweat-slick skin, he was acutely aware that she only wore a sports bra and yoga pants. "Give it some time and it will all come back."

"I don't have time." She looked away. "I heard from my agent today. I've been invited to dance at a wedding next month. A very glamorous one for a millionaire."

His wife should have better assignments. She should star in movies instead of dancing to old songs. "You'll be ready."

"I wasn't their first choice," Tina continued. "A famous actress was supposed to do it but she dropped out. My agent won't tell me who the original dancer was but I have a feeling she's a big name."

"The guests won't know," Dev said in an encouraging tone as they continued to sway to the hypnotic beat of the drums. "And they won't care once you start dancing."

"Thanks, Dev," she said shyly. "I know dancing at

weddings is frowned upon with Bollywood royalty. It's just another way to make money, but I enjoy it."

"More than acting?"

"Dancing is my first love. I got into acting because acting paid more money." She gave a small frown. "What about you? Do you enjoy acting?"

"No one has ever asked me that before." It had always been assumed that he would go into the family business.

"You're very good at it. A natural. But then, you're a natural at most things."

She said it as if it was a character flaw. "I'm more interested in the business behind the camera."

"I know. I've seen how excited you get with the new technology and the new markets. But if you're bored with acting, you should retire and focus on what you love."

"Give up being the king of Bollywood?" he mocked.

"King?" She chuckled. "You are a prince at best. And not the only one."

Dev's smile widened. He could always trust Tina to give her real opinion. She was supportive but she always gave her real opinion. There weren't that many people in his life who would do that.

She glanced at the clock. "I have to get ready for Nikhil's party."

"Need help with the sari?" he teased as Tina walked away.

She glanced over her shoulder and smiled. "I'm not wearing a sari."

"What happened to the devoted and adoring wife I was promised?"

Her smile turned bittersweet. "She's long gone."

The dance club was exactly what she needed. It was dark and crowded with colorful lights flashing on the floor.

She lifted her arms and shouted her approval at the DJ when she heard the first few notes of her favorite song.

Tina felt Dev behind her. She leaned against his solid chest as he wrapped his arms around her waist. She'd forgotten how much fun she used to have dancing with Dev.

Nikhil had a very exclusive guest list but the only person she really noticed was her husband. And he couldn't keep his hands off her. She was secretly pleased at how his eyes had widened when he saw the silver dress she had decided to wear. Tina could tell he approved of her short strapless dress. His gaze would settle on her curves and she noticed he hadn't said a word about changing into a sari.

Did Dev know that she had chosen the dress for him? Tina realized she had to stop thinking like that. She stepped away and twirled out from his embrace. She needed to stop thinking like a wife. A full-time, long-term wife. She needed to start distancing herself.

She stumbled to a halt when Dev grabbed her wrist and drew her close. She gave him a questioning look as he guided her off the crowded dance floor. He was frowning and his mouth was a straight line.

"What's wrong?" she asked over the music.

"You were wobbling again," he said with a grim expression as he escorted her to a small table in the very back of the club. "Sit down and I'll get you something to drink."

"I'm okay, Dev." She reached for his hand and held him still. "I want to go back in and dance."

"No, it's not like you to lose your balance," he said. "I want you to rest."

"There is nothing wrong with my stamina or my strength," she insisted.

"I'll decide that."

She tossed her hands in the air and sat down next to the table. "Why are you being overprotective?"

"Why can't I look after you?" he said in a growl.

"Why can't I look after you?" she shot back.

Dev jerked his head back in surprise. "I don't need looking after."

"But I do?" This was the problem of being married to a traditional man.

He leaned forward, his hand on the back of her chair. "You've had a rough year."

"So have you." And she hadn't been there for him when he needed her the most.

"Why won't you let me take care of you?" Dev's eyes flashed with anger. "Why does this always have to be an argument?"

"You help more than enough." He helped her so much that she felt like she couldn't reciprocate. "I live in your house, I spend your money and I don't contribute anything."

"Contribute? You do more than you realize. When we were preparing for our son, it was the first time I felt like I belonged to a family."

The familiar ache settled in her chest when he mentioned their son. "Anyone can give you that."

"You'd be surprised," he whispered in her ear. "Anyone would take what I have to offer. But you reject everything I do for you."

Her shoulders stiffened and she turned her head sharply to stare at Dev's dark brown eyes. "I don't reject you."

"Yes, you do." This time Dev looked away. "You reject every gift I give you, every gesture, every act I make outside the bedroom."

Was that true? Tina nervously licked her lips as she

tried to remember. She had felt uncomfortable when he lavished her with gifts and she couldn't give him anything in return. He could make her life easier with just one phone call and all she seemed to do was make his life a living hell. "I don't mean to. It's just that…"

He turned quickly, his gaze holding hers. "What?"

Tina gestured between them. "We're unequal. You have all the power and I have none."

She saw the shock tighten Dev's harsh features. "That's how you see it?"

"That's how it is!" she insisted and leaned closer. "How can I accept help from you when I can't give anything back?"

"You help your family," Dev pointed out. "Your mother and sisters. You don't expect anything in return."

"Well, that's different because—"

"Because in your family, you're still trying to make up for the fact that you were a financial burden to your mother."

Tina bit her lip as her skin flushed. She felt exposed. She hated feeling that way, but most of all, she hated that Dev knew.

"And you'll keep working every job you're offered," he continued, "and you pay for everything your family needs because you feel like you have to pay a debt."

Tina wanted to look away. How did he see all this? What else did he notice? "My mother could have gotten rid of me once my father left. She had considered taking me to an orphanage," she said as her voice cracked. "Instead she kept me."

"And you're a financial burden to me?" he asked. Dev slowly shook his head. "Just how much money do you think you spend?"

"It's not how much I spend. It's how much I *cost* you.

You could have ignored me and the baby. You married me because you felt like you should. And what did you get out of it? Your career still took a hit once you got married."

"I don't care about that."

"You will one day." If he didn't care about it now, it was because he didn't know how it felt to be at rock bottom. Soon he was going to resent the trouble she caused. Tina slowly rose from her seat. She couldn't discuss this anymore. Maybe she was as fragile as Dev thought. She felt like she needed a few minutes alone.

"Excuse me, I need to find the restroom. No, no." She held out her hand as he rose to escort her. "Don't worry, I can find my way there myself."

"I'll get you a drink while you're gone."

"Thank you." As she walked to the restroom she admitted to herself that she did feel a little wobbly. It might be the stiletto heels or that she needed to drink some water.

Stepping into the dark room with black sinks and counters, Tina glimpsed her reflection in the mirror. Just as she suspected, she looked like a wreck. With a heavy sigh, she combed down her spiky hair with her fingers and readjusted her dress. She stepped into one of the stalls and closed the door. Once she locked it, she rested her head against the cool metal and gave a deep sigh.

Tina frowned when she heard a group of women enter the restroom. She just wanted some peace. Wait until the ache eased in her chest and Dev's words stopped swirling in her head. All she needed was a few moments to regroup before she returned to the party.

"Did you see Dev and Tina?"

Tina lifted her head. The unmistakable voice of

Khushi, the playback singer, was coming from the direction of the mirrors.

"You'd think they were on their honeymoon," Prisha complained. "I mean, come on. Get a room."

Tina rolled her eyes at the choreographer's comment. She was never demonstrative with Dev in public. The reason had more to do with a code of conduct for Bollywood stars than her private nature. One didn't embrace, kiss or show any overt affection. She didn't even graze lips with her costar on-screen because it would offend many moviegoers.

"From what I understand, the honeymoon will end in five weeks," Khushi drawled. "And then they are getting a divorce."

Tina skin went cold as the blood roared in her ears. Had she heard Khushi correctly? How had she known about the secret agreement she had with Dev?

"What?" Prisha screeched. "Where did you hear this?"

"Shreya."

Tina exhaled as her hands began to shake. How did Shreya know? She must have heard a rumor, but there was only one source she could have got it from.

"What else did she tell you?" Prisha asked excitedly.

"Tina agreed to stay for two months and she will get to use Dev's connections in return. I knew that woman had married him for her career. Didn't I tell you?"

Tina closed her eyes as her stomach gave a violent twist. They knew everything. And there was only one way Shreya would have gotten this information. Dev had told Shreya everything.

CHAPTER TEN

TINA STOOD VERY still as the realization hit her hard. She couldn't breathe. Couldn't think. She felt sick. Dizzy. She pressed her hands on the metal door as if it could hold her upright. It seemed like ages before Khushi and Prisha finished repairing their makeup. Once they left the restroom, Tina took several moments before she exited the stall.

Tina glanced at her reflection in her mirror. She looked pale and wounded. She wanted to believe Dev hadn't betrayed her, but she couldn't think of any other explanation. She tried to think of how Shreya could have got this information but the images of the tabloid pictures flickered in her mind.

She slowly walked to the door, her movements awkward and choppy. Her stiletto heels skidded against the floor and she righted herself abruptly. She really didn't think Dev would have shared that information with anyone.

Tina squeezed her eyes shut before the burning tears spilled from her lashes. She had believed Dev when he said he had been faithful. He had been hurt that the only reason she returned was because of the pictures. She had heard it in his voice and had felt it in his touch when they had fallen into bed.

But if he had not been sleeping with Shreya, how did the other woman know all the details?

Tina walked out of the restroom and she cringed at the loud music bombarding her sensitive nerves. The frenetic lights and the wild dance movements were suddenly too much for her. She had to get out of there. She needed to think. Run. Hide.

"Tina?" She heard Dev's voice right behind her. "Where are you going?"

She kept moving, staring at the exit with laser focus as if her life depended on it. "I have to get out of here."

"Why? What's wrong?" Dev was suddenly in front of her, forcing her to stop. She was tempted to push him away but he was stronger than she.

She didn't want to tell him. She wasn't ready for this confrontation. The tears were shimmering in her eyes and the pain was howling through her, threatening to break free. If he had betrayed her confidence like this, she didn't know how she was going to survive.

Every instinct told her to protect herself. If she told him what she knew, he would come up with an excuse. And she would believe him because she wanted to. She needed to get away before he could totally destroy her. But she had to see his face. If she surprised him with what she knew, he wouldn't be able to hide his guilt.

"There were some women in the restroom who were sharing some juicy gossip," Tina said weakly, her throat aching as the emotions clawed at her. "They knew about our agreement. Every last detail."

Dev grabbed her shoulders and bent his head so he could look directly into her eyes. "What are you talking about?"

"Shreya told others about our agreement. She knows that this marriage is going to end in five weeks."

Dev's dark brown eyes narrowed into slits. "That's impossible," he said in a growl.

Was it? Dev said he hadn't had an affair with Shreya, but what if he had shared his thoughts, dreams and problems with the other woman? What if he had talked to her about things he hid from his wife? "I don't know what she's going to do with the information." Tina's voice shook.

"What are you trying to say?" His fingers tightened against her bare arms. "Do you still think I'm having an affair with Shreya?"

"No, but I think you confided in another woman about something private, something just between us."

Tina couldn't take it anymore. She leaned forward and rested her head against his shoulder. She felt Dev's muscles tense with surprise before he gathered her in his arms and held her close. She sighed when he cupped the back of her head with his large hand. For a moment, she felt safe.

"Let's go home, Dev," she pleaded softly.

"Not yet," he said as she stroked her hair. "I need to do something first. *We* do."

She lifted her head. "What are you planning?"

"Follow my lead." He encircled his fingers around her wrist and guided her to the dance floor.

Tina didn't trust the urgency in his tone. "No, no, no." She dragged her heels. "Not until you tell me what you want to do."

He looked over his shoulder. "For once, we are going to face this as a team. A united front. That was our mistake in the past."

United. They hadn't been partners, hadn't shared a life together, since they got married. "What are you talking about?"

"We are husband and wife but we lead separate lives. We didn't grieve together and we didn't help each other after the miscarriage. That stops now. We are going to start by attacking these rumors together." He squeezed her hand. "Are you with me?"

It meant giving him total control and allowing him to lead. It meant trusting him. Believing he wouldn't throw her to the wolves. It meant taking a leap of faith and ignoring every instinct that screamed for her to run and hide.

Tina gave a sharp nod. "Let's do this," she said and was rewarded with Dev's bold smile.

Dev led her through the dance floor. She watched as the crowd parted for him. Tina's shoulders tightened as her husband approached the DJ's platform. She couldn't predict what he was going to do. Call out Shreya and her friends? Tina clenched Dev's hand in warning. She felt too vulnerable.

Her heart banged against her ribs when Dev held out his hand to the DJ and silently motioned for the microphone. The DJ didn't question the request and immediately handed it to him. Tina knew nothing good could come out of this. She wanted to drift into the crowd but she had promised Dev that she would follow his lead. She had no idea it would be this difficult.

"DJ, I would like to dedicate a song to my wife."

Tina went very still as the crowd roared their approval for the romantic gesture. If only it were genuine, Tina thought. She tried to relax under the spotlight as Dev gathered her close. He gave her a look of pure adoration that took her breath away.

"This woman said yes to me almost a year ago. She gave me the pleasure—no, the *honor*—of becoming her husband. I don't know what I would have done without her."

Tina ducked her head as a blush crawled up her neck and flooded her face. Did Dev know that this counterattack was the most precious gift he had given her? Wearing the Arjun jewels had been a stroke of genius. It gave the illusion that he considered her worthy of the family name. But this…this declaration from a Bollywood megastar meant something more. Dev was demanding high society respect his wife, making them believe she had power and influence over the mighty megastar. That he was wonder-struck by her.

"I realized I haven't said it enough. I didn't show this special woman how I feel about her every day." His voice was rough with regret and sincerity. "But I'm going to correct that mistake now."

Tina heard a few women in the crowd sigh at his words. She would have sighed, too, but this was pretend. Part of the fantasy. A ruse to stop the rumors.

"My wife is everything I want. Everything I need. I'm grateful that Tina is willing to share her life with me. So, DJ, I feel like celebrating. Play us a slow song."

The guests clapped and whistled as Dev returned the microphone. The lights in the nightclub dimmed as the first notes of a saxophone played. Dev drew her to the middle of the dance floor and gathered her gently in his arms.

She sensed the other guests finding dance partners and swaying to the music, but she was only aware of Dev. How her soft breasts pressed against his hard chest and how his large hands spanned across her hips. They moved in unison effortlessly.

Tina couldn't look at Dev. He was a good actor. Better than her. If he captured her gaze, he would see how much she wanted those words to be true. How much she wished he had included words like *love* in his speech.

Tina pressed her head against his chest and closed her eyes. A sigh shuddered through her body when Dev cupped her head with his hand. The tenderness made her weak in the knees. When he placed a kiss against her hair, Tina wanted to hold on to this moment. Make believe it was real, just a little while longer.

When the music stopped, Tina reluctantly pulled away. She was an emotional wreck. She felt raw and exposed. "Let's go home now," she suggested.

Dev wrapped his arm around her as he guided her off the dance floor and through the club. He didn't say a word as they exited the lobby. He cradled her close while he called for the car and fell silent again. Was he regretting his speech?

She didn't object as he bundled her into the backseat as if she was a delicate treasure. She didn't say anything until she noticed he wasn't getting into the car with her. "What's going on?" Her eyes widened as she realized he was staying at the party. "You're not coming with me?"

"I saw Shreya at the party and I'm going to find out how she got this information," he said. His voice was calm but she saw the anger in his eyes. "She needs to learn that you are my wife and I will protect your reputation."

"But—"

"Take her straight home," he told the driver before he closed the door.

"Damn it, Dev," she said through the thick glass. But he had already turned away and entered the nightclub like a warrior heading in for battle.

When was he going to realize that the rumors would persist, Tina wondered as the car pulled away from the curb. Nothing they said or did would change that. Their hasty marriage and her brand image made her a burden.

The only way to minimize the damage was if Dev distanced himself from her. He needed to cut her loose.

He needed a drink.

He needed more than that, Dev decided as he swung open the front door of his home and headed straight to his bedroom. What he really needed was Tina. He needed her to believe—really believe—that he wouldn't do this to her.

The house was dark and quiet. Empty. The silence tore at him. It was the last thing he wanted to feel as the fury still rushed through his blood. He had walked into an eerily quiet house like this for the past four months and he wasn't willing to do it again.

He climbed up the steps two at a time. Dev was going to make Tina listen to him. He was going to convince her once and for all that he didn't want Shreya. He didn't want anyone but his wife.

Dev strode into the bedroom and stopped abruptly when he discovered Tina wasn't there. His anger flashed white-hot at the thought that she had moved into one of the guest rooms. He swung around and marched to the nearest guest room. If Tina was trying to make a statement by leaving his bed, she had picked the wrong night.

The bedroom was undisturbed. Something close to panic mixed with his anger and it was a volatile combination. He slammed open the door to the next guest room and he found it empty. He systematically checked every room on the top floor as the urgency pulsed through his veins.

Had she left? Fear, cold and hard, twisted in his stomach as he hurried down the stairs. Was this one truth too hard for her to swallow? He had to admit that the evidence was building up against him.

As he hurried through the drawing room and the massive dining room that had held so many parties, he heard a strain of music. Dev lurched to a stop, listening. The song was familiar. It was from one of Tina's favorite romantic movies.

He pivoted on his heel and walked straight to the kitchen. He faltered to a stop when he saw Tina. The relief crashed through him so hard that he slumped against the door frame.

She was barefoot but still wearing her silver beaded dress. She leaned against the granite counter as she watched *Dilwale Dulhania Le Jayenge* on the TV mounted on the other side of the wall. Shahrukh Khan and Kajol were embracing while standing in a field of yellow flowers. It took him a moment to notice the small coral-colored pot on the stove. He inhaled the scent of *khichri,* the simple comfort food of rice and legumes.

Tina had cooked? This was the first time he had seen her cook since she had returned. It had been something she had enjoyed but she'd lost interest after the miscarriage. He wasn't sure what it meant now. He wanted to see it as a positive sign but he knew to tread lightly.

"You're still here." His voice came out rough and low.

She jerked and looked around. The small plate in her hand held a mound of *khichri* tinged yellow with turmeric. She scooped up the rice and legumes with her fingers and carried it to her mouth. "Where else would I be?"

Her mother's house. A hotel. Another country. Anywhere but here. He slowly approached Tina, unable to read her mood. Uncertain about his welcome.

"You want some?" she asked, holding the thick rice with the tips of her fingers.

He shook his head. That wasn't the question he had expected to tumble from her lips. What was going on?

"I didn't tell Shreya about our agreement," he said. "She had overheard us in the courtyard the night you returned."

Tina slowly lowered her hand and placed the rice back on the plate. She stood still for a brief moment. "I should have known."

Dev reared his head back. "You believe me?" He had thought he was going to have to convince her. Get on his knees and beg for her to listen.

"Yes," she said as she reached for a cloth napkin and briskly cleaned her hands. "I'm not going to lie. I first believed you told her. I almost didn't discuss it with you."

"I'm glad you did." Tina trusted him enough to confront him with the information. She had stayed and waited for his return. That had to mean something. "Shreya has also learned her lesson."

Tina lifted her chin and watched him carefully. "What do you mean?"

"She is no longer working under the banner of Arjun Entertainment," he said grimly.

"You canceled her contract?" Tina eyes widened. "Why would you do that? She is a bankable star."

"She needed my studio more than we needed her."

"Her family is powerful and influential. This is going to cause you so many problems."

"You seem to forget, Tina. Shreya spread gossip about you. About my *wife*. About an *Arjun*. I will not tolerate that. Soon everyone will know that there will be consequences if they disrespect you."

Tina tossed down the napkin and braced the edge of

the counter. "I think your display of adoration fixed everything."

"I hope so." It wasn't a display. He had meant every word.

Tina frowned as she warily studied his face. "It was convincing. Maybe too convincing."

"What do you mean?" he asked. Did she have a problem with his words? With the idea that he adored her?

"It's going to bring up more questions when we divorce in a few weeks," she said, looking away. "Who's going to believe what you say after that?"

"I'm not worried." If all goes to plan, they would still be together.

Tina pressed her lips and gave a shake to her head. "Thank you, Dev. I liked having you rush to my side."

He gave a slow, shy smile. "You're welcome."

"Next time, give me more of a heads-up on what you plan to do."

"I will." He took a step closer until he caught a hint of her perfume.

Tina nervously licked her lips. "We make a good team. I think we should keep doing that. Show that we are partners in every way."

He narrowed his eyes at her matter-of-fact tone. "What are you talking about?"

"It's not enough for your investors to hear that you have a stable family life. We have to demonstrate it. Show the world that our...marriage is an unbreakable force."

Dev wasn't sure if he should trust this offer. Not too long ago she'd seen him as the enemy. "Why would you want to help me?"

"Because it will make you happy." She darted her gaze away.

She wanted to help him. Make him happy. There was

only one thing that would make him happy but he didn't think she would agree to forever. But did this mean that she no longer saw him as the enemy? "Everything has changed."

Dev was right. Tina curled her toes against the cold linoleum as she considered what he had said. Everything had changed between them. He had made it clear that he demanded everyone respect her. He protected her. Protected *them*. That's all she needed to know to stay until their agreement ended.

"We should still sleep in the same room." She was trying to sound blasé but her voice was high and rushed. "Servants talk, you know."

"That Sandeep is a chatty one."

She pursed her lips to prevent a smile. "So we should remain in the same bed."

"If you think that's best," Dev drawled.

"I do," Tina said. She glided her hands over her hips and allowed her fingertips to brush against the short skirt of her dress. She was so nervous. She wasn't sure what words were coming out of her mouth. All she knew was that she wanted to take her husband to bed. But would it feel too much like a reunion? A fresh start?

Dev gave her a speculative look and she felt the thrill of exhilaration.

What were the consequences of seducing your husband? She didn't know. Dev had been the enemy for so long. For months she'd felt like she had to hide from him. Protect herself from her husband. But now she knew the truth. He didn't take control over her life to punish her. He cared about her. At one time he may have loved her.

But he was still dangerous. He made her want things that weren't good for her. He clouded her mind with desire and made her believe in love and forever. She wanted to stay with him, stay as his wife, even if it meant giving up everything. Her freedom. Her peace of mind.

"I want to help you," Tina told him. And it was the truth. She wanted him to have everything he desired. She moved to set the plate in the sink, her body straining, and she felt Dev's gaze linger on her high, full breasts.

Tina slowly straightened as the sexual power pulsed through her. She gently swayed her hips to the music playing on the TV. Dev seemed mesmerized. She knew she had him caught and a dangerous thrill zipped through her veins.

Dev was very still. Her stomach clenched when she saw the glint in his dark eyes. She shouldn't tease a man like this.

"I have the power to make your dreams come true. If you let me." Her words were rushed as excitement coiled tightly around her chest.

She saw his harsh features tighten with desire. The air between them crackled. Now it was time to make her move.

"It's been a long night. I'm going to bed. Are you going to join me?" she asked innocently. Her legs shook slightly as she took a step closer. She forced herself to remain still as her leg bumped against his.

He leaned forward and she found it hard to breathe. Her heart was pounding in her ears and her legs shook. An electric current sparked inside her, pressing just under her skin as he grasped the edge of her short dress.

"Are you inviting me?" he asked. His big hand brushed along her thigh.

"Yes-s-s." Now she was a little afraid that he was going to accept her proposition. Scared, because this night with

Dev would change everything. She was sharing his bed not because she had to, but because she wanted to.

Dev didn't remove his hand. She felt his fingers flex and she knew he wasn't as unaffected as he appeared.

A quivering tension wrapped around them. She knew Dev was tempted to bunch her dress in his fists and strip her bare. And she wanted him to do it.

Dev slowly moved closer, as if waiting for her to change her mind. To run and hide. Tina's anticipation was thick and heavy. She felt as if she would burst out of her skin.

Tina raised her head, jutting her chin as he towered over her. He stood so close that she could feel his body heat and inhale the faint scent of his cologne.

He lowered his head and kissed her. Dev gently explored her lips but she sensed he wanted to claim her mouth. Claim her. He wanted to capture her and press her against him.

She wanted more, too. His soft kisses teased her. Her pulse raced and her skin tingled with need. Tina parted her lips as she stepped closer into his embrace.

Dev gave an appreciative moan as he dipped his tongue past her lips. Her kisses grew urgent as her heart pounded against her chest. Her breath hitched when his large hands skimmed her bare skin.

Tina pulled away. Her lips felt swollen and she wanted to burst out of her tight, hot skin. She looked up at Dev and took a step back.

Dev looked fierce. His touch might have been gentle but he couldn't hide the male aggression that darkened his eyes and pulled at his harsh features. His chest rose and fell with each uneven breath.

And he still didn't grab for her. No matter how much he wanted to. He was allowing her to set the pace.

Her gaze held his. He looked hopeful. Uncertain. Tina reached for his hand. His fingers imprisoned hers. As if he was afraid to let go.

"Come with me," she said in a whisper and guided him out of the kitchen.

CHAPTER ELEVEN

As SHE FLATTENED her hand against the closed door of the bedroom, Tina paused. Was she ready for this?

Dev pulled his hand away and braced his hands on her hips. She closed her eyes and shivered as his breath warmed her neck. She was unprepared for Dev to span his hands against her waist. Tina gasped as he slid his fingers along her rib cage before cupping her breasts.

She sagged against him as the wicked sensations slammed into her. Her breasts were full and heavy. Her nipples tightened painfully. Tina arched into Dev's hands as he tugged down her strapless dress.

Dev's groan vibrated against her neck as he caressed her bare breasts. Her legs trembled when he pinched her nipples. Pleasure, hot and piercing, forked through her. She let out a high cry as a dew of sweat bathed her skin.

"How do you do this to me?" Dev asked roughly in her ear. "I can't keep my hands off you."

She felt the same way about him. She wanted to beg for more. Plead for Dev to take her breasts in his mouth. She rolled her hips as the lust coiled tight in her belly and she felt his arousal against her.

Tina wrenched open the door and drew Dev into their bedroom. Light from the hallway streamed into the darkness. Once they reached her bed, Tina turned around and clasped her hands on Dev's angular face and blindly sought his mouth with her lips.

Her kisses were wilder and she found it difficult to slow down. She didn't know what made this different than all the other nights. Why the urgency clawed at them. This wasn't their last night together but in some ways it felt like a rebirth.

Dev pulled her short dress down her hips and kicked it away. She was very aware that she was almost naked while he was fully dressed.

"Take off your clothes," she muttered against his lips.

His fingers tightened against her skin. "Take them off for me," he whispered.

She reached for him with barely concealed eagerness and pulled his shirt over his head. While Dev kicked off his shoes, Tina gave a playful push and watched him tumble onto the bed. She squealed with surprise when he grabbed her and took her with him.

His husky chuckle died as she straddled him and explored his solid chest with her hands and mouth. She liked how his muscles bunched under her exploratory touch and how he hissed when she scratched his flat nipple. Tina felt powerful. Desired.

She reached for his belt and suddenly she was underneath Dev. This was where she liked to be. She was surrounded by him and nothing else existed. Nothing else mattered. Tina stopped trying to regain her position as he captured her nipple with his mouth. She went wild as the white-hot pleasure streaked through her.

Tina rolled her hips as Dev dragged her panties down her shaking legs. She couldn't take much more of this. Her sexual hunger was ferocious and the insistent ache in her pelvis made her want to scream.

"Now, Dev."

"Not yet," he said in a steady voice as he rubbed his fingers along the folds of her sex.

His touch wasn't nearly enough. "Please," she said in a broken whisper. "I need you inside me right now."

She nearly sobbed when he withdrew his hands from her. Tina squeezed her eyes closed and heard the rustle of his clothes and then the tear of foil. She opened her eyes and saw him put on protection.

That was a sharp reminder. Tina's breath caught in her throat as she watched him. They weren't starting over. They weren't dreaming of a family anymore. This was the beginning of the end.

Dev settled between her thighs. Her stomach twisted with excitement when she felt the thickness of him against her. He clamped his hands on her hips and he entered her with one long thrust. Tina's gasp echoed in the large room when Dev roughly tilted her hips even more. The most amazing sensations stormed her.

"More," Tina whimpered as she bucked her hips against Dev. He responded with a slow thrust. Tina thought her eyes were going to roll back from the dizzying pleasure.

She wrapped her legs around Dev's waist. He groaned as her tight flesh gripped him like a fist. His pace grew faster, each thrust deeper, as she followed the ancient rhythm.

The pleasure consumed her. She begged for more as she clung to Dev. She wasn't sure what her body was chasing, what it was reaching for until the sensations exploded.

Her mind went blank as she climaxed. Her lungs burned and she forgot to breathe. She held on to Dev as he growled something fierce before he found his release.

It took her a few moments before she realized Dev had

gathered her in his arms. She laid her head on his chest and heard his pounding heartbeat. She stared at him, stunned and shaken.

She was falling for him again. Falling in love with her husband. Had she ever really stopped loving him? The fear threatened to choke her. Tina knew she had to be careful. But how could she when she went wild in his arms every time and then craved his protective embrace?

Tina knew she couldn't get used to this. If she stayed she would lose all her freedom. Dev would have total control of her. Her emotions. Her life.

She couldn't let that happen again.

"Tujhe dekha to yeh janna sanam…" Dev sang softly the next morning as he strode into the bedroom after his shower. One towel was draped low around his hips while he dried his hair with another. He paused when he realized he was singing the romantic song that had been playing in the kitchen the night before.

Damn, what kind of power did Tina have over him? All she had to do was take him to bed and he was breaking out into song. If he wasn't careful, he'd start dancing. But he couldn't hide the satisfaction that poured through his veins or the hope that wanted to burst from his skin. His relationship with Tina had taken a turn and he was so close to his goal. He would keep her as his wife long after their first wedding anniversary.

Dev stopped toweling his hair when he thought he heard a whimper. He glanced at the bed. Tina was huddled in the middle with the twisted bedsheets cocooned around her.

"Tina?" Was she having another nightmare? She'd said she didn't get them anymore. Dev rushed to the bed and saw that she held her hand over her face. It wasn't a bad dream. She would thrash and kick out. Scream. At the moment she didn't seem to have the energy to move. "Tina, what's wrong?"

She grimaced and scrunched her eyes closed. "I don't feel well."

He remembered she'd had a stomachache last night. He'd thought it had been from the stress of dealing with Shreya. Tina was rarely ill and she hadn't shown any signs of pain during the night.

"Was it the *khichri?*"

She opened one eye. "My *khichri* heals stomachaches, it doesn't create them."

He smiled at her offended tone. No one questioned her cooking. "Did you have anything at the party?"

"No."

He tried to remember what she'd had the day before. She had visited her mother but he remembered the number one rule with Reema Sharma's cooking: avoid it at all costs. Tina would know that. She once told him she'd learned how to cook as a matter of survival.

But there was one thing Tina couldn't refuse when she visited that side of Mumbai. "Did you eat street food when you went to your mother's?"

"Of course I did," she said as she wrapped her arms around her stomach. "They have the best *chaat.*"

He placed his hand on her forehead. She looked pale but her skin wasn't warm to the touch. "What did you have to eat?"

"Samosas," Tina said and swallowed hard, as if the thought made her nauseated. "And *channa chaat*. I also had some of Meera's *dahi puri....*"

He shook his head. "And you wonder why you're not feeling well. If they were anything like the *chaat* stalls we've visited, you probably have food poisoning."

She gradually opened her eyes. "I don't think it's the food."

He didn't know what else it could be and he wasn't going to take any chances. Dev knew he was being over-protective but he hated seeing Tina in pain. "Come on," he said as he reached for her hands. "Let's get you to the doctor."

She flinched and jerked back to avoid his touch. "No!"

He stared at Tina as her voice echoed in the large bedroom. He saw the hunted look in her dark eyes and the fear etched across her face. She was shutting him out again.

"I see," Dev said as he slowly straightened to his full height, the pain radiating from his body. The hope shriveled inside once he realized nothing had changed between them.

"I don't want a doctor," she said quietly, unable to meet his gaze. "I hate hospitals."

"No," he corrected her, his voice cold and stiff as the biting hurt slashed his chest, "you don't want *me* to help you."

"That's not it."

"You don't want my name or my protection. My connections? Yes. My concern? No." Dev's tone was harsh. "Now I'm not even allowed to look after you when you're sick?"

Tina weakly closed her eyes. "I don't know why I did that."

"I do." She was rejecting his help again. Rejecting him. "You trust me when I tell you I didn't have an affair with Shreya. You trust me enough to share your bed, your body. But when it comes to taking care of you, you can't trust me at all."

"It was just a reaction," she explained. "I wasn't thinking about it."

That made it worse. Dev clenched his jaw as he fought
back the rising tide of anger.

"Go back to sleep, Tina," he said wearily as he took a
step away from the bed. "I'll have Sandeep bring something up for you. He'll check up on you throughout the
day."

"Where are you going?"

"Out." Any other time, he would have thought she
sounded like a wife. But he knew the concern wasn't
for him.

"Dev?"

There was something about her tone that pierced
through his anger. Dev stopped at the bathroom door
and looked over his shoulder. Her back was turned away
from him. It was a familiar sight. "What is it, Tina?"

There was a long pause before she spoke. "Would
you...stay...with me? Please?" she asked. She said the
words slowly, as if they were dragged out from her. "I
want you to look after me. No one else."

It wasn't true. She'd rather curl up in a dark corner
alone than ask for help. Dev knew she was doing this for
him. And yet she acted as if she expected he would reject
her. What had he done to make her think that?

"Yes, *jaan*," he said as he walked to the bed. He didn't
feel victorious. He felt as if he was walking on eggshells.
One wrong move or wrong word, and he could ruin everything. "I'm here for you."

Hours later Dev set down his laptop computer and leaned
back in his chair. He gave Tina an assessing look. "You
are a terrible patient."

"So I've been told," Tina said as she flipped through

the movie magazine Dev had asked Sandeep to buy. She sat on the bed and wore her softest, most comfortable *shalwar kameez*. Her stomach didn't hurt as much but her heart was heavy with regret. She couldn't rid the memory of Dev's stricken expression from this morning. She kept pushing him away when she really wanted him near. She didn't know how to stop.

"You don't need to stay, Dev," Tina said with a sigh as she tossed the magazine to the side. "I had some bad *chaat,* that's all."

"You shouldn't try to diagnose yourself," Dev warned her. "You should have a doctor check you out."

"No, that's not necessary." She shivered at the thought. She had grown to hate the sight of surgical scrubs and white coats. "I'm fine. Why don't you go watch cricket or something?"

Dev propped his chin against his hand. He was in no hurry to go anywhere. "Why are you trying to get rid of me?"

Tina leaned her head back against the stack of pillows behind her. "I already feel bad that you're wasting your day in that chair staring at four walls."

"This is where I want to be," he said softly.

"I don't know why," Tina muttered.

"If I was sick, would you look after me?"

She made a face and looked away. "Yes, but that's different."

"Because you never want to rely on anyone," Dev said. "You have to do it all yourself."

It was true. She wasn't comfortable asking for help. Not from anyone, especially her family. She had already been a burden to her mother. A problem for her husband. The last thing she wanted to do was highlight why she was an inconvenience.

"Next time I'm not going to wait for permission to take care of you," Dev said. "I don't mind that you need me. I like it when you depend on me."

Tina frowned. A great many people relied on Dev, from his mother to the people who worked for him. He didn't need another dependent. "You don't want to take on my problems, Dev. You have enough of your own."

"I don't see it that way," Dev said. "When you disappeared, I frequently dropped by your mother's house to check on her and your sisters. You weren't around so I did it for you. Your family is my family."

"Family is important to you." It was a fantasy of his to be part of a big, noisy family. Have the kind he saw in the movies but never had for himself. That was yet another thing she couldn't give him.

"I like being a big brother to Rani and Meera," Dev said with a hint of a smile. "I like helping your mother. She treats me as a son instead of a movie star. I would like to take care of you. You need to stop fighting me every step of the way and just let it happen."

"It's not that easy." She had given him that control, had placed all of her trust in him because she couldn't function. It had been terrifying. And then suddenly he had no longer been there, choosing to be anywhere but at her side. She had felt betrayed.

"Because I wasn't there when you miscarried. I wasn't there afterward."

She raised her gaze to the ceiling. "I didn't ask you to be there."

"I should have been there even if you were trying to kick me out of the room." He paused. "Why didn't you ask for me? Why were you pushing me away? Did you think that I would turn away? Reject you when you needed me the most?"

Tina pressed her lips together as the tears burned in her eyes. "Yes," she said.

The tense silence pulsed in the room. "What did I do to make you think that?"

"It wasn't you. My father ran out when we needed him the most," Tina said softly, lowering her gaze. "When life wasn't turning out the way he thought he deserved it. But he had been absent long before that. I learned not to ask him for anything because it would only lead to disappointment."

"I didn't run out on you. I made sure you had everything you needed." Dev met her gaze. "But it's my deepest regret that I wasn't there when you needed me the most. It wasn't until you disappeared that I realized I was following my parents' footsteps. They were too busy making movies. Sandeep was there for me more than my parents. I don't want to be an absent husband or father. Next time, I'm going to every doctor's appointment and I'm sitting at the table every night for dinner."

Next time. Tina closed her eyes. Next time wouldn't include her. She knew Dev would be a good father. She would've loved to have seen him cradling their baby. He would be a fierce protector, a patient teacher and offer the unconditional love he hadn't got as a child.

She opened her eyes when she heard the beep of his watch. "Time for your medicine and a drink," he announced as he pushed a button on his modern timepiece before rising from his chair.

"No more water." She shook her head. Dev was taking his role as caregiver very seriously.

"You need to keep hydrated," he said as he walked around the bed to the door.

"Be careful, Dev. I might get used to this kind of attention."

He paused and captured her gaze. "That's the plan."

Tina watched wordlessly as he strolled out of the room, whistling a tune from a Salman Khan movie. She stared at the door long after he left. She wasn't sure what he'd meant. Did he want her to stay after the two months were up? No, she shouldn't get her hopes up. His words must have had a simpler meaning. That the next time she was sick, she should turn to him for comfort.

There was probably not going to be a next time. She was usually healthy. She couldn't remember the last time she'd had a cold or the flu. The last time she'd felt nauseous and dizzy was...

Tina's gasp echoed in the bedroom. She flattened her hands against her stomach as the panic raced through her blood. The last time she'd felt like this was in the very early stages of pregnancy.

"No," she whispered as the fear clawed through her. "No, no, no! Not again."

CHAPTER TWELVE

TINA LEANED HER head against the tile wall of her bathroom and closed her eyes. She was sick with nerves. She wanted to double over as the panic threatened to consume her.

Flapping her hands at her sides, Tina tried to gather up the last of her courage. She hadn't been feeling very brave for the past two weeks. Not since she realized her stomachache could mean she was pregnant. Tina had been in denial ever since.

She refused to be pregnant. Refused to go through that nightmare again.

But she couldn't ignore the symptoms anymore. She continued to fight the dizziness. The nausea came in waves. Her appetite increased and her sex drive was out of control.

Dev didn't seem to notice or mind her symptoms. He liked how she reached out for him while they walked side by side. She held on to him, at times clung to him, relying on his strength while her world tilted. He enjoyed sharing his food with her, coaxing her closer as he fed her by hand. Dev never missed the opportunity to stroke her lips with his thumb or capture her chin so he could steal a kiss.

And the sex…Tina's breath hitched in her throat as

her skin tingled. She couldn't get enough of Dev and he reveled in the knowledge. Encouraged it. It was as if he knew the sight of his bare chest and the scent of his skin drove her wild.

Tina rubbed her eyes with the heels of her hands and groaned. She couldn't be pregnant. She and Dev had been careful. It didn't matter if they made love in the court-yard under the stars or indulged in fast and furious sex that took them both by surprise. Dev always used pro-tection. Except for that one time...

She was probably pregnant, Tina admitted to herself. She pressed her trembling lips together as the fear spiked in her chest. She wanted to be a mother, but what if there were complications? What if she miscarried again? The tears trickled down her cheeks. What if she slipped into the darkness, but deeper, and this time never resurfaced?

Dev would take care of her. The thought whispered through her troubled mind. Her eyelashes fluttered as she remembered his promise. He would be there for her this time. He would care for and protect her and the baby. She knew Dev would honor his vow.

And he would insist that they stay married. Tina shook her head and sighed when the hope bubbled and fizzed in-side her like champagne. She still loved her husband and wanted to stay with him. But not this way. She wouldn't trap him into marriage again.

Tina wiped the tears from her cheeks with the back of her hands and pushed away from the wall. Perhaps she was borrowing trouble. It was possible that she wasn't pregnant. That her body was still recovering from the stress and changes she had suffered in the past year.

She clung to that belief as she cautiously approached the sink and grabbed the slim pregnancy test stick. Tina braced herself as she glanced at the screen. For a moment her mind didn't register what the two pink lines meant.

Pregnant.

She was pregnant. Tina tossed the stick back on the counter as if it had burned her. A sob erupted from her throat and she clapped her hand over her mouth. It was happening all over again. He legs shook and she slowly slid to the floor. She knelt on the cold linoleum as she cried. What was she going to do? She couldn't lose another baby.

Tina didn't know how long she had been in that position when she heard a hard, authoritative knock on the bathroom door. Her throat was raw and her body ached. Her eyes felt red and swollen. She already felt broken and her journey had barely started.

"Tina?"

She jerked when she heard Dev's voice. She swung her attention to the door as the handle jiggled. He could not come in here. Not when she was vulnerable and needy.

"I'm fine," she lied, her voice wobbling. She forced herself on her feet and glanced at the mirror. She looked horrible. Her skin was tearstained and blotchy. She quickly turned on the faucet and sluiced cold water on her face.

"What's wrong?"

Tina hesitated. A part of her wanted to tell Dev. She was tempted to lean on him and share her deepest fears. But was that wise? Would he take control of her life again?

She had to keep this a secret, Tina decided as she grabbed a towel and patted her face dry. For now. Until she was properly seen by a doctor and understood everything she was facing.

Something heavy slammed against the door and the

solid wood shuddered under the weight. Tina whirled around when she heard Dev's urgent tone from the other side. "Tina, open this door right now."

She looked around the bathroom and found the pregnancy test stick was still on the counter. Her fingers fumbled as she snatched it and threw it in the waste bin. It was blinding pink. She grabbed a few tissues and wadded them as the wall rattled behind her. Tina tossed the bunch of tissues in the waste bin and hurried to unlock the door.

She swung the door open and her gaze clashed with Dev. His dark eyes were wild, his skin stretched taut against his harsh features. He towered over her, the worry and relief pulsating in the air. She noticed he held his shoulder as if it ached.

"Dev—" She faltered into shocked silence as he lowered her arm that blocked his entrance and peered into her bathroom.

"Why didn't you open the door when I asked?" His words were clipped with anger as he grabbed her hands. She instinctively tried to pull away but he was too strong. Dev turned her palms over and checked her wrists.

The old scars on her skin suddenly felt hot and red. "I told you I don't cut anymore," she mumbled. She wished he couldn't see those signs of her weakness.

He glanced up but didn't let go of her hands. "Why were you crying?"

She bit her lip and looked away. "Dev, it's perfectly natural to cry. It's a release from stress and—"

"Not the way you were crying," he said gruffly. "It was as if your whole world was ripped apart."

She swallowed hard. "I'm not going down the rabbit hole again. I promise."

"I think we should stay home."

"Stay home? No, that's not necessary." She blinked

as she suddenly remembered they were supposed to go to a wedding today. The daughter of a business associate was getting married in a huge three-day event. All of Bollywood was attending. Tina wasn't ready to face the pomp and pageantry, but it was better than staying at home and avoiding Dev's probing questions.

She felt Dev watching her intently and the silence was almost unbearable. Tina struggled to meet his gaze. She was taken aback when she saw the pain in his eyes. It was just like when he had told her that he had gone through hell with her. She didn't want him to go through it again. This was her battle.

He didn't need to suffer with her. Because of her.

The *mehndi* celebration was bigger and bolder than Dev had expected. The prewedding ceremony was traditionally to prepare the bride for the wedding. Now it was a huge party that was almost as extravagant as the *walima*.

The ballroom was decorated to give the impression that they were in an ornate tent. Gauzy white curtains and tiny strings of light were draped from the ceiling. The heavy scent of flowers couldn't mask the aroma of the rich, spicy food. He glanced at the circular platform in the middle of the room. The future bride sat next to her groom as they watched a dancing troupe perform.

He noticed that despite the luxurious surroundings, the bride followed tradition and didn't wear makeup or jewelry. Her hands and feet were decorated with intricate henna designs and she wore a simple mustard-yellow gown with a dark green veil over her hair.

The guests were a mix of Bollywood stars and members of the Hindi film industry. They were more interested in the other guests than the proceedings. This was exactly what Tina hated about the wedding extravaganzas of his contemporaries.

Dev looked around the crowd, searching for his wife. He wished she had stayed at his side. He liked linking his hand with hers, but she kept finding an excuse to part.

She was creating a distance between them and he was getting worried. Dev's eyes flicked across the white-and-gold ballroom. Why had she been crying earlier today? It had been more than crying. It had been gut-wrenching sobs that had torn at him.

Instinct had guided him when he'd tried to break down the bathroom door. Dev rotated his shoulder as he felt a twinge of pain. He had panicked but this time he knew not to dismiss the signs.

This time. Dev pulled uncomfortably at his tie. Was she falling into a depression again? Was this arrangement triggering it? No, he decided. He refused to believe that.

Tina might think he had overreacted, but for the past two weeks he had noticed a change in Tina's behavior. She had been listless and staring off into the distance. He had woken her from a bad dream the night before and soothed her back to sleep only for her to talk in her sleep. Why wasn't she telling him what was troubling her?

Dev's heart clenched when he found Tina. She stood among a circle of friends, tilting her head back as she laughed. He yearned to hear that sound more than the chime of her bangles or the faint jingle of her gold anklets.

She didn't wear the sari he had suggested. Dev thought she looked feminine and graceful in a sari but he had to admit she was incredibly sexy in the emerald green *ghagra choli*. The short sleeves emphasized her toned arms and the snug shirt revealed the smooth, golden skin of her midriff. The long beaded skirt flared at the knee, but it wasn't as modest as he had hoped. Instead it clung lovingly to her curves.

Tina looked strong and healthy. Elegant and stunning. He was damn proud to have her at his side. As his wife.

Dev's expression grew fierce as he watched Tina. He was proud of her. She had achieved so much through hard work and perseverance. She didn't seem to be aware of her own strength. Not only had she faced challenges to support her family, but she had also struggled to recover from grief and illness.

He saw Tina's posture stiffen before she raised her head and captured his gaze. She gave him a questioning look and Dev allowed his eyes to linger on her tiny blouse and bare stomach. He dragged his gaze back to her face and watched his wife blush.

Her smile faded as he approached. She quickly said something to the other women and briskly met him in the middle of the ballroom.

"What do you think of the wedding?" Dev asked.

She glanced at the round stage. "I feel sorry for the bride."

Her words pinched his chest. He grabbed at his dark tie and loosened it. Was this her opinion on marriage? Did she feel sorry for all brides and wives? "Why is that?"

Tina gave a small shrug. "It's supposed to be her day but no one is paying attention to her. Not even the groom. They are all too busy trying to do business and make deals."

Dev placed his hand on the small of her back and was rewarded with the touch of her warm, smooth skin. "I paid attention to you at our wedding," he said against her ear.

Tina shivered from his nearness. "Yes, but I made sure there were no other distractions."

Their elopement had been stripped down to the essentials. He had ignored the postwedding rituals that included welcoming Tina into his house and his family. His wife was modern but he should have honored her new role. He should have shown how important she was to him.

"I'm sorry how I acted," he said as they walked outside the ballroom.

"On our wedding day?" Tina frowned. "What are you talking about? You were very solemn during the ceremony."

"I was arrogant when I asked you to marry me," Dev admitted. He stopped on the red carpet and looked at the ropes of lights coiling around the pillars at the entrance of the party. It was quiet and there were only a few servants walking around. "I didn't ask or propose. I told you that we were getting married."

Tina pulled away and stood in front of him. "What's going on? It's not like you to be this...introspective. How many drinks have you had?"

"I'm not drunk. I was thinking about when we first got married. You were my wife but I treated you like a guest in my home, in my life."

Tina gave him a look of concern and rested her hand on his arm. "It's okay, Dev. If I had a problem with that, I would have spoken up."

"No, you wouldn't. You were afraid to make waves. Cause any inconvenience."

She dropped her hand and looked way. "You make me sound like a coward."

"Coward? You?" He scoffed at the idea. "You wanted everything to be perfect even if it required you to make the sacrifices."

Tina crossed her arms. "I'm not a martyr."

"You're too independent," he complained with a growl. "You refuse to ask for help."

"I'm working on that." She took a step back and he followed.

"Why don't you audition for one of my movies?" Dev asked. Her insistence on avoiding Arjun Entertainment was like a thorn in his skin.

"No! You still don't get it, Dev." She thrust her hands in her short hair and gave a harsh sigh. "Everyone wants something from you. If they don't ask for it, you'll offer something. Anything. It's how you work a relationship."

Dev narrowed his eyes. He didn't like where this conversation was going. "What are you talking about?"

"You think you have to do something to earn your way into people's hearts," she said as she gestured wildly with her hands. "You have to be number one in the box office to win approval from your parents. You have to pay everything to gain acceptance with my mother."

Was this how Tina saw him? That he had to buy his way to a person's heart? "I have money and I want to help out."

"At first I thought it was your way of maintaining control in a relationship. Now I realize that you can't just give yourself. You don't think you're enough."

He didn't like this. He jutted out his chin as the dark emotions started to swirl in his chest. "That's not true."

"And you are just as reluctant to ask for help as I am." She placed her hands on her hips. "Do you realize that asking me to stay for two months was the only time you asked for my assistance in anything?"

"You were pregnant and then you were grieving." He had gone out of his way to keep the world at bay. He didn't want her to worry about anything.

"I still wanted to look after you. You were my husband."

"I *am* your husband."

"I ask for your advice all the time," she continued as if he hadn't made that declaration. "But I didn't want you to think I married you because you could help my career. I wanted you, not what you could do for me."

"You didn't need to prove anything," he said. "I know why you married me."

Tina's cheeks went red. "You do?"

"You didn't want to be a single mother."

Tina blinked and gave a slight shake of her head. "Dev, I didn't marry you just because I was having your baby."

Dev clenched his teeth as the curiosity swelled inside him. Why had she married him? He wanted to know but he was afraid the reason no longer applied. What would it take for her to *stay* married?

"This is the problem with attending weddings," Tina said as she cast a look at the entrance. "It makes you think about your own. Your marriage. What you would have done differently."

"You know what I would have done differently?" he asked gruffly.

She gave him a wary look. "No, Dev. What?"

"I wouldn't have gotten you pregnant."

His words were like a punch to the chest. If she hadn't gotten pregnant, he would still be the most eligible bachelor, living a carefree life and driving his career to new heights. "I know," she said softly. "It changed everything, didn't it?"

"No, *jaan*. You misunderstand me." He reached out and gathered her in his arms. She pressed her hands against his muscular chest and felt the solid beat of his heart. "I would have protected you better. I would have looked after you."

"That was my responsibility, not yours." She should have been more careful but apparently she did not learn from her mistakes.

"I disagree." His expression was fierce and she watched the fire in his eyes. "I should never have allowed you to get pregnant. It was an oversight on my part. But I was glad you were carrying my child."

Her heart did a funny, slow flip. She knew he had been excited about the baby but she needed to hear that he didn't regret it. "You always wanted a family."

"And I wanted *you*," Dev said quietly. "I would have eventually asked you to marry me, but the baby moved up my timetable."

Her heart skipped a beat. "You would have married me even if I wasn't carrying your baby?" That she did not believe. He was idealizing their affair. If she hadn't been pregnant, he would have ended their affair to enter an arranged marriage with Shreya.

"You gave me the one thing I never had," Dev said as she brushed his finger along her cheek. "A home life. A world outside the film industry."

"You could have gotten that on your own," she whispered as her throat tightened with emotion.

His mouth lifted in a lopsided smile. "Not without your insistence."

She rested her forehead against his chest, unable to look at him. She felt shy. Uncertain. She had fought for him to have a life outside the office, but she didn't feel like she had made any significant achievement. "You really don't ask for much," she muttered.

"I asked for everything. And I got it."

And then I lost it.... The words hung above them unspoken. Dev rested his hand against the crown of her head.

"You're the one who didn't ask for anything," he pointed out.

"That's because I would ask for the impossible. What purpose would that serve?"

"I can make anything happen."

She smiled at his arrogant statement. He was confident of his abilities but she knew there were some things even the great Dev Arjun couldn't achieve. She wanted to ask for another chance. Try to save their marriage with no time limit. She wanted to stay but she knew nothing had changed. She couldn't risk her future with a man who would strip her of her voice, her power and her financial independence, believing it was for her own good.

"What do you want right now?" he whispered. "Ask and I will give it to you."

She wasn't going to ask for the moon or the stars. She wasn't going to ask for her heart's desire when she knew it wasn't going to happen. Instead she focused on what she could have for now.

"I've had enough of this wedding." Tina lifted her head, her gaze ensnaring his. "I want to go home and take you to bed."

His smile turned wicked. "I'm all yours."

CHAPTER THIRTEEN

TINA STIRRED IN her sleep, burrowing her head against Dev's shoulder as the blanket slipped down to her waist. She felt as if she should remember something but the memory was just out of reach. She stretched, murmuring with delight when her breasts pressed against Dev's chest as her legs brushed against his.

A small smile formed on her lips as she dragged her foot along his calf. She enjoyed the friction of his rough hair against the side of her toe. Tina felt the solid muscle and strength under his warm skin. She liked waking up next to him this way. Naked with their arms and legs tangled, as if they couldn't stand the idea of letting go in their sleep.

She'd have to get used to waking up alone again. Tina's smile faded as she slid her hand down Dev's rock-hard abdomen. According to their original agreement, she only had a few more days of this—a little more than a week.

Tina didn't want to think about it. She tried to block it from her mind as she brushed her fingertips along Dev's hip, noticing how he didn't stir under her touch. She wanted to wake him up and make love. Lust heated her blood at the thought. She didn't want to waste a minute of the time they had left together.

She was almost embarrassed at how eager she was to

be with her husband. It wasn't too long ago when she had looked for every possible way to stay out of his bed. At the beginning of this deal, she had started a countdown, telling herself that she could get through the two months. Now it was a reminder that this was all going to end and she would have to accept a life without Dev.

She wasn't ready, Tina thought as she wrapped her hand around his erection and sighed. She wanted another chance at her marriage. A do-over.

She could have it if she told Dev about the baby. But she couldn't do that to him again. She couldn't keep him in this marriage because she was pregnant. She couldn't let him take over her life. She knew he was doing it out of a sense of duty, protection instead of punishment, but it was a fate she couldn't accept.

Tina knew she had to tell Dev about her pregnancy. It was the right thing to do and he deserved to know, she decided as she slowly stroked him. Her instincts told her to wait until he no longer had legal power over her. It wouldn't be that many more days before she moved out. Today was the fifteenth and…

The fifteenth. Tina froze, her hand clenched around Dev's velvety soft skin as the shock rippled through her. Today was her wedding anniversary.

Her eyes flew open. Her heart was beating fast, her throat tightening as her gaze collided with Dev's.

She knew. Dev was aware of the moment she realized it was their wedding anniversary. His breath caught in his throat as he watched the myriad emotions flickering in her brown eyes. Not one of them was celebratory.

Did she still think this marriage was a failure? He wasn't ready to give up. Tina was the only woman he wanted and he was going to convince her to stay.

It's a shame she wasn't pregnant, Dev decided. That would give them a bond that could never be broken. Not only would they create the family they wanted, but the nine months would also give him plenty of time to repair their marriage.

Tina looked away. "Why did you stop?" he asked in a husky growl.

She turned. "We should get up."

Dev moved swiftly, covering her body with his, before she could get out of bed. "I was thinking…"

"This early in the morning?" she asked, doing her best not to make eye contact. "That's never a good thing."

"Why don't we take a trip?" he asked as he kissed a trail down her throat.

"A trip?" There wasn't a hint of interest in her voice.

"We could visit the beaches in Goa," he suggested as he brushed his lips along her breastbone. "Or we could visit the foothills."

"Don't you have a few upcoming meetings at the office?" she asked. Her breathing was uneven as she rocked her hips in anticipation.

"I can postpone them," Dev offered absently as he slid his mouth down her stomach. His pulse kicked hard as he hooked Tina's legs over his arms.

"You shouldn't have to," Tina said huskily as she twisted her fingers in his hair. "I know you have a lot riding on these investors. We don't need to go anywhere."

He paused, wondering why she was acting this way. In the past, they had gone on trips together for work. Why would she decline when it was for just the two of them? "We haven't been anywhere since Los Angeles."

Her body jerked. "That was a disaster. Why would you want to try again?"

"Why not? Let's replace a bad memory with a good one."

"I'm sorry I walked out on you," Tina whispered. "Can you forgive me?"

"I already have." And he meant it.

She gave a tight-lipped smile. "You were right. I was so lost in grieving that I pushed you away. I thought you had married me because of the baby. I wasn't sure how you really felt about having me as a wife."

He was also at fault and he was trying to make up for it. Dev wanted to show how much he loved and appreciated her. He wanted to give her the honeymoon she'd never had but he was reluctant to mention that. She was avoiding the topic of their anniversary and now wouldn't be a good time to present her with the jewelry set he had bought that had once belonged to a *maharani*. It was the bridal jewelry she should have had.

"Where would you like to go?" He bent his head and teased her navel with his tongue. "Europe? Australia?"

"I'd like to stay here," she said breathlessly.

He pressed his lips on her inner thigh. "I can take you anywhere in the world and you want to stay here?"

"Why not?" she murmured as she bucked her hips. "Can you think of a better place?"

"No," he said as he pressed his mouth against the slick folds of her sex. The only place he wanted to be was at home with Tina.

"Why don't you wait for your husband in his office, *Tinaji?*" Dev's assistant, dressed in crisply ironed white *kurta shalwar,* escorted her into the garish office. Tina flinched at the sight of the gold-trimmed furniture and campy movie posters. "His meeting should end soon."

Tina gave the older man a knowing smile. Dev was

never on schedule. She was lucky if he showed up within the hour.

"It's a shame he had to work on your wedding anniversary," the assistant said.

"It's not all bad. Dev loves what he does," Tina replied as her courage slowly faded. "But I thought I could steal him away and take him to lunch."

"You should visit more often. He would love that. Can I get you anything to drink?"

She declined, the tension rising in her as she waited in the silent room. She didn't know how Dev could work in this office. It wasn't like him at all. He preferred natural textiles and modern art. Everything here celebrated his family's cinema achievements. It was a constant reminder of his family's legacy.

Tina bit her lip as she looked around. She tried not to compare her modest success to that of the Arjun family. She had made mistakes and taken the wrong advice. While she may never be a Bollywood megastar, she was taking steps to take full control of her career.

And sometimes she needed to take a step away from work. Right now she needed to focus on her family, not her career. *I can do this...I can tell Dev about the baby... This is a good thing...Dev is going to be thrilled, just like last time.*

Only last time, he hadn't thought about what all could go wrong. Neither of them had. Tina slowly sat down on the sofa. Last time he had embraced the news. In his world, everything he touched turned to gold and every choice he made turned out better than expected.

Stop it. You can't hide this anymore. No more excuses. It was time to tell him. Why not now, on their wedding anniversary? Dev cared about her and she had to trust him. Tina knew he would take care of her if anything went wrong and she had nothing to fear.

Tina tugged at her pink sari and made a face. She hated wearing it but she liked how Dev responded when she wore the feminine garment. She needed all the help she could get to place him in a receptive mood.

She looked down at the pile of this week's movie magazines on the coffee table in front of her. A few of them had the Arjun family portrait, commemorating Vikram's long career. Another magazine cover caught her eye. Her stomach clenched when she saw a picture of Dev and Shreya in an embrace.

Why? Why did they have to show these pictures and share these stories on her anniversary? How many "it won't last" or "trouble in paradise" stories must she suffer through?

Tina reached out for it and stopped. She didn't want to know. She wasn't going to read the article or the headline. What purpose would it serve? If she kept reading the gossip it would chip away at the trust she had in Dev. If he said he was not having an affair with Shreya, she would believe him. She wouldn't require proof, just like he trusted her when she swore she hadn't slept with anyone during their separation.

"Tina?"

Tina closed her eyes when she heard the familiar voice. What was her mother-in-law doing here? How could she have forgotten that Gauri Arjun had an office suite in the building?

She reluctantly turned around and saw Dev's mother enter the room. The older woman was stunning in a vibrant green sari. Her hair flowed smoothly against her shoulders and it was all Tina could do not to smooth her own short, spiky hair. What was it about this woman that always made her feel awkward and insignificant?

Tina rose from her seat and adjusted her sari as she politely greeted her mother-in-law. The woman waved away her attempts impatiently.

"What is this about you going to Hollywood?" Gauri asked. "This is unacceptable. The Arjun family is the face of the Hindi film industry. Going to Los Angeles is a betrayal of our heritage and our culture."

Tina's eyes widened as she jerked in surprise. "Who says I'm going to Hollywood?"

"The rumors are everywhere that you are going to star in a television show. An Arjun on American television!" Gauri shuddered. Tina wasn't sure which part of the American television it was that bothered her.

But why did Gauri believe she was... Tina winced as she remembered the tidbit of information she had shared with her mother. The casual remark the television director had said at the treatment center about how they should work together. Nothing was signed or agreed upon, but that didn't matter. Reema was going to make it look like Tina was in high demand. This was yet another indication for Tina that she needed to get another manager.

"Now is not a good time to discuss this, *Maaji*," Tina muttered as she nervously clasped her fingers in her lap.

"My son isn't going to Hollywood," Gauri said in a hiss. "His destiny is here."

Tina frowned. "Who says he's going to Hollywood?"

"You are his wife. You go where he goes. Unless..." She reared her head back. "What are you saying?"

"I believe she is saying that I'm not invited." Dev drawled. Tina whirled around to see Dev leaning at the door. Her heart stopped for a moment when she saw glittery coldness in his eyes. "Congratulations on the role."

Why would he think she had a role? A role she hadn't even discussed with him. A role that would require leaving Mumbai. Leaving him.

Did he think she would do that without talking to him? Of course he would. She had left him like that in the past. But she was different now. They were different. Why didn't he see that? "Dev, let me explain."

"There's no need," he said as he strode to his desk. He showed no emotions but Tina could tell by his choppy movements and the muscle bunching in his jaw that he was holding back his fury. "You are getting the career that you've longed for, leaving behind the husband you no longer want and settling a few scores before you leave. Am I missing anything?"

CHAPTER FOURTEEN

THE SILENCE PULSED in the office after his mother muttered something and left. Dev felt the tension coiling inside him, so swift and ferocious, that he was surprised his body didn't shatter. She had used their marriage—used him—as leverage to further her career. He never thought Tina would betray him like this.

He rested his fists on the desk and forced himself to look at his wife. "My publicity department is in a panic," Dev said. "It appears that your mother is shopping around a tell-all exposé."

"My mother?"

"Not only will it discuss how horribly I treated you and how amazing I am in bed, but it will also explain your mysterious disappearance."

"This is the first I've heard of it," she blurted out. "You know I would never do something like this."

"Do I?" he asked silkily as the anger ate at him like acid. "And yet you threatened me with this not too long ago. At the time I didn't believe it. I didn't think you had it in you."

"When did I say that?" She tilted her head as it occurred to her. "Wait, do you mean when I found out that Shreya was playing Laila? I said that in anger but I wouldn't do that. That would have hurt me just as much as you."

Dev stared at her. It would have been suicide to her career if she had planned to stay in Mumbai. Now she was ready to throw a grenade on everything they had together and walk away. Tina's action proved only one thing: she didn't want another chance at this marriage.

The blow was staggering. He had done everything he could and she was ready to walk. Why had he thought he could change her mind? She had not mentioned a future together.

"Say something," Tina whispered. She watched him with extreme caution as she wrung her hands together.

"You're a better actress than anyone gives you credit for," he said as he pushed away from his desk. "I believed you."

She frowned as she nervously tugged at her sari. "What are you talking about?"

"You refused to take my name because you didn't want anyone to accuse you of marrying an Arjun for career advancement." He braced his legs and crossed his arms, ready for battle. "You refused to work with me or with Arjun Entertainment. You rejected my help every step of the way because you didn't want to feel obligated to me."

"I was wrong to do that," she said. "I didn't know that my decisions hurt you."

Was that it? Or was she playing the devoted wife for another reason? There had been starlets who had wanted to be part of the Arjun dynasty. They had been traditional with perfect backgrounds, but none of them interested him. Had Tina known how to seduce him? Was she just as devious as the characters she played?

Her career would skyrocket if she didn't play the dutiful wife. Salacious gossip—true or false—would put her in higher demand. But it was a short-term strategy. If she played it right and cashed in quickly, she would have the money and fame she'd always wanted.

"I take it you saw the magazine cover. The one with me and Shreya."

"I don't care about that." She gestured at the magazine on the coffee table.

"Don't lie to me, *jaan*. I know that you saw a divorce lawyer today." He had seen the amateur pictures on a few blogs moments ago in his meeting with the publicity department. The publicist was annoyed that these pictures had been taken on their anniversary. Dev had been stunned. It had been like a sharp dagger to the heart. All this time he had thought they were reconciling but Tina wasn't going to wait one minute longer to start the divorce process.

Tina gasped. "Divorce lawyer? What are you talking about?"

"You must have rushed right over there after seeing the magazine." She'd sworn she would walk out if there was any evidence that he was having an affair. "Or did you make the appointment two months ago when we made our agreement? Or was it longer ago than that? When you walked away? The night after we got married?"

"You've got it all wrong, Dev."

He tried to ignore her stricken expression. "You married me to improve your career in Hindi films. Now you're going to Hollywood and you don't need my help."

Tina took a step forward. "I married you because I loved you."

Dev scoffed at her declaration. "I don't believe that for a second. If you had loved me, it was a very weak love. It broke the moment we faced trouble."

"That's not true. I have always loved you." She squared

back her shoulders and pressed her fists at her sides. "Do you know how demeaning it is to love someone who resents being married to you? Or how much it hurts to love someone who makes you feel unwanted and unworthy of his attention?"

"It wasn't too long ago when you declared that you hated me."

"I hated what you did to me." Her chin wobbled as the tears shone in her eyes. "I hated that you had all the power and I had none. I hated that I could love you even under all the hate."

All the power? He was defenseless when it came to Tina. "Get out." His voice was weak and raspy.

Tina went very still. "What?"

"You heard me. Get out." He pointed at the door. "Get out of this office. Get out of my home. Get out of my life."

She clasped her hands together and gave him a pleading look. "Dev, I didn't go to a divorce lawyer."

"Move out of my house immediately and go to America." He needed her to go across the world. He would breathe easier knowing she couldn't invade his life again.

"But...but..." Tina looked at the door and then at him. "What about your investors?"

He gave a humorless chuckle and rubbed his hand over his face. Once he had felt guilty about lying to her. He knew she would be angry when she found out but he'd thought it was for a good cause. His crumbling marriage. "There are none."

"What? I don't understand. What happened?"

"There never were investors. I lied, Tina." Dev watched the realization dawn on her. "I said that so you would stay. I had this crazy idea that if I could have you back home for a few months, you would fall back in love with me and we could start over."

Tina closed her eyes and pressed her lips together. "Wh-why didn't you tell me that?"

"Right, because you were so receptive to the idea. You would have run as far as you could in the other direction if you'd known what I wanted."

"Dev, you have to believe me. I didn't do anything behind your back. I want to—"

"I've heard enough." That was the problem. He wanted to believe her. He wanted to believe that he misunderstood. That Tina was innocent. And he would keep on believing as she wrung the hope out of him. This time he had to protect himself. "Get out."

She stared at him. He felt the wild energy swirling around her. An urgency. He knew the feeling. It had happened the last time his world fell apart and there was nothing he could do to save his dreams.

"I mean it, Tina." He watched her tremble at the menace in his voice. "If you don't leave right now, I will carry you out myself."

"But..." she gave another quick glance at the door. "What if I'm pregnant?"

Her words stung like the tip of a whip. His anger spiked so hot that it felt incandescent. Dev decided Tina was lucky there was a desk between them. "Don't even joke about it."

"I'm serious. What happens if I'm carrying your baby?"

"Life wouldn't be so cruel."

She gasped and jerked back. He knew his words wounded her. It didn't please him.

"If you're pregnant, I would stay married to you," he said. Only this time, he wouldn't hope for a reconciliation. "We will have separate homes, live on different continents and have separate lives. It worked for my parents. Why should I want anything different?"

"No." She shook her head. "No, you don't want that. I know you, Dev."

But that was before he'd discovered that Tina didn't want a future or a family with him. How long would she have dangled the promise of forever if the American television deal hadn't gone through?

"And the child would stay with me," he said. He couldn't imagine the demands she would have made if she had carried his child. The Arjun heir.

"No court would allow that!"

He didn't know why they were arguing about it. Tina had made it very clear that she didn't want to carry a baby again. Namely, *his* baby. That had hurt him more than he cared to admit. "Do you think you can fight the influence and money I have?"

Tina blinked as she swayed on her feet. She grabbed the back of the chair as her body began to shake. "You wouldn't," she whispered.

He didn't think he would, but he wasn't thinking about what was right or wrong at the moment. He was in pain and he was lashing out. "Don't test me," he warned. "But you're not carrying my baby. This time I walk away. This time *I'm* asking for the divorce. Get out of my life, Tina. I don't want you as my wife anymore."

The drums pounded as Tina spun wildly on the stage. She was giving this performance everything she had. Her lungs burned, her legs shook and she fought the wave of dizziness. She was almost done.... Almost there...

As the music ended with a dramatic flourish, the folds of her tunic still moving, Tina smiled and tossed her hands up in the air to thunderous applause. She wanted to savor this moment, the last time she was going to perform, but the crowd's reaction didn't break through the sadness that had settled around her the past month.

Tina curtseyed to the bridal party and immediately left the stage, ignoring the cries for an encore. She waved to the well-dressed crowd and gave a deep sigh as her lungs threatened to shrivel. She knew this wedding dance was her last performance. She was retiring after tonight.

"I don't think anyone noticed that one mistake." Her mother was at her side wearing her best *shalwar kameez*. The *dupatta* shot with gold thread was barely hanging on to her shoulders. She gave Tina a bottle of water and a hand towel to wipe off the sweat. "And what happened at the end when you stumbled? Are you feeling dizzy again?"

"It'll go away," Tina said. She had overdone it and it was going to take a moment or two to recover.

Reema glanced over Tina's shoulder as if gauging the audience's mood. "After tonight, I'm sure you will get other offers to dance at weddings."

"I'm not interested." Her fingers fumbled as she tried to open the water bottle.

Reema sighed. "You should keep your options open. I understand why you refused the tell-all. It wasn't my best idea."

"That's why you're no longer my manager," Tina reminded her. "You should have told me what you were planning to do before you shopped it around."

"It's easier to ask for forgiveness than permission," Reema said. "And it's a shame the American TV deal didn't go through."

"There was never a deal, Amma."

"No one needs to know that," Reema said. "But that

doesn't mean you have to turn your back on entertaining altogether."

"There's no point in starting up again only to have to stop in the next few months." Her hands brushed against her stomach. "I want to concentrate on getting through this pregnancy."

"Or are you trying to hide your pregnancy from your husband?" Reema asked.

"You know why I have to hide this information," Tina said tightly. When she had moved in with her mother and sisters, Tina told them how she had sought help for her depression. She had hoped to find support but their responses had been awkward and uncomfortable. At times she wished she had kept it a secret.

"I think he should know," Reema said as she hurriedly fixed her *dupatta*. "He should be the one taking care of you."

"I am taking care of myself and I am under the care of the best doctors. Also—" Tina's voice faded as she watched her mother's gaze dart over her shoulder again. "What's going on?"

"Going on?" Her mother's voice was high and screechy. "Nothing."

She sensed a stir of interest in the workers behind her. Dread twisted her stomach as she watched the guilt bloom in her mother's face. "What did you do?"

Reema thrust her chin out defiantly. "I invited him to Meera's wedding. He's still paying for it after everything that happened. And I might have let it slip—"

Tina gasped in horror. Dev had found out about the baby. "No!" She whirled around, her head spinning. It took a moment for her eyes to adjust. She blinked and stared into Dev's dark brown eyes.

Her heart leaped and crashed when she saw his fury.

He towered over her, his hands clenched at his sides. He was an intimidating sight in his dark suit and tie. Her balance weaved as she inhaled a faint whiff of his cologne. She wanted to throw herself in his arms and she wanted to run far, far away.

"It is true?" His voice slashed through the tense atmosphere.

"I…" She frowned as dark spots gathered in the corner of her eyes.

"Just tell me the truth." He reached out and grabbed her upper arms. "Are you carrying my baby?"

The dark spots grew bigger and she suddenly felt very cold. "Dev?" she called out before her head lolled back and she fainted.

Tina didn't want to wake up. For the first time in a month she felt warm and safe. She snuggled deeper into her pillow and sighed. There was something strangely familiar about the bed. It was more luxurious than the one at her mother's house. And the buzz of the ceiling fan reminded her of a different room. A different bed.

She forced her eyes open and looked at the fan whirring above her. Her chest tightened and she decided she wasn't brave enough to look to her side. She remembered fainting at the wedding and waking up in Dev's strong arms. She had struggled to keep her eyes open but lost the battle. When she had opened them again she had been in a car, still surrounded by Dev's arms.

Now she was back in Dev's bed. What was going on?

She jerked when she heard her mother's loud voice down the hall. Reema was complaining and giving orders. Some things were normal.

"I wanted to take you to the hospital."

She froze when she heard Dev's voice. Damn. She

paused to gather all the courage she could muster and turned to see Dev lounging on the chair next to the bed. His jacket had been discarded and his tie was loosened. His hair was mussed as if he had raked his fingers through it continuously. And he still looked incredibly handsome.

"But I know how you feel about those places," he continued. "So I brought you here and we're waiting for the doctor."

"I don't need a doctor." She needed to get out of here. Get out of Dev Arjun's sphere where he ruled all.

Dev's eyes narrowed with impatience. "Don't make me regret this decision, *jaan*. The only reason we are here is because of your fear of hospitals."

"I'm not afraid of hospitals," she insisted. She had been going to doctors and specialists since she left Dev a month ago and the hospital settings didn't bother her. "It just brings back the bad memories."

"You didn't answer my question," he reminded her. "Are you pregnant?"

He knew. She was displaying the same dizziness as the first time she was pregnant. He didn't need confirmation so why did he keep asking? "You don't want the answer."

"You don't know what I want."

"I know that you want me out of your life. You think life couldn't be that cruel to have me carrying your baby. But I don't know why you, who wanted to end this marriage as soon as possible, haven't made a move towards a divorce." His lack of action had surprised her. Confused her. Made her hope for things that weren't possible.

"Because I don't want a divorce. I never did."

She scoffed. "You did when you thought I was giving a tell-all interview. You thought I was betraying you. Hurting you so I could further my career."

He tilted his head in acknowledgment. "I was hurt and I said a few things I shouldn't. What I should have told you, what I should have said a year ago, is that I want you as my wife."

It was too late for her to hear those words and yet they pulled at her. "Don't waste your time revising history," she whispered as her chest ached with regret. "You're only saying this because you think I'm pregnant."

"I want this child, too." He leaned forward and braced his arms on his knees. "I want the family life that I thought only existed in the movies. You made my dream come true and I want to hold on to it forever."

"I want something else," she said, her voice rising. He was saying all the things she wanted to hear and it scared her. Her heart was beating frantically and yet she was settling deeper into the bed when she should be launching out of it and running out the door. "I'm going to Hollywood, remember?"

"No, you're not," he said softly. "I know all about it. When you refused to go to Los Angeles, your mother came to me in a panic. She thought I was trying to control your career again."

Tina wanted to scream with frustration. She didn't think her mother would have said anything to Dev. She wanted him to think she had moved on so she could get through this pregnancy without any interference.

"You didn't think I had an affair with Shreya, did you?"

Tina frowned as she tried to think of an explanation that didn't reveal too much. "I know nothing is going on between you and Shreya." The magazine headlines bothered her because she knew the truth. She didn't like the lies that were said about Dev and wanted people to know that he was a man worthy of her love and respect.

"I was sure you were canceling our agreement on our anniversary," Dev said. "I thought you didn't trust me. It turns out I had jumped to conclusions and ruined everything."

"I trust you, Dev," she whispered.

"If you're pregnant, you can't get rid of me," Dev said as he held her gaze. "I will be there for you whether or not you want me around."

"You don't have to go through this again," Tina said. "Get out now while you can."

"I don't want to get out," Dev said in a growl. "I want to care for you. I protect what is mine."

"I am not yours." It hurt to say that out loud. Tina blinked away the tears that threatened to spill from her lashes. "You threw me out, remember?"

"I felt like I was the only one fighting for us. I wanted you to fight just as hard. Instead, you walked away."

Tina's deep sigh dragged from her throat. "I'm tired of fighting."

"So I'll keep fighting for us," he vowed as he watched her intently. "But if I can't have that, then let me support you. Let me be a part of this."

She wanted Dev to be part of every step in this journey. She needed to rely on him if something went wrong. But if he knew what could happen, why was he volunteering to stay? "You've been through this before. Why would you want to go through it again?"

"Is that why you're not telling me? Is this your way of protecting me? Or were you keeping the baby a secret so I didn't take it away from you?"

"Does it matter?"

"Yes, it matters!" He swore and lowered his voice. "I love you and I want to look after you. Why is it so hard to accept that?"

"You love me?" she repeated in a daze.

"Yes, I have always loved you." He looked away, almost shyly. "I tried to fight it, but it overpowers me. I thought that the love I have was strong enough that it could carry the both of us. I was wrong. I want you to love me. Trust me. Need me."

She hesitated, feeling like she was on the edge of a big cliff and ready to take a leap of faith. "Dev, did you wonder why I went to your office a month ago?"

"I thought you had come back from the lawyers and were going to ask for a divorce."

Her skin felt hot as nervousness raced through her veins. "I was going to ask for you to give our marriage a second chance."

He winced. "You were?"

"I wore a sari, Dev. That should have been your first clue that I was going to ask for something important."

Dev leaned back in his chair and rubbed his hands over his eyes. "You wanted to try again. And I threw you out."

"I want you as my husband," she said, her heart pounding against her ribs. If he rejected her now she wouldn't recover. "But not for a limited time. I'm staying with you through thick and thin. If you don't want this, you need to tell me now."

"Tina, you are what I want, and I will show that to you every day."

EPILOGUE

Four years later

Tina Sharma Arjun strode to the front door of her home as the hot, fragrant breeze pulled at her shoulder-length hair. She tilted her head when she heard the loud, pulsating *bhangra* music.

"Memsahib!" Sandeep greeted her as he stood at the threshold.

"It sounds like the party has already started," she said with a smile.

"They are in the courtyard," the manservant said as he accepted her bag. "How did the filming go today?"

"It was wonderful," Tina replied. She felt energized even after a full day of shooting an item number. She had always wanted to be an item girl, who made a cameo appearance in a song-and-dance scene. When she casually mentioned it to Dev, he had made sure she got the honor to be featured in the latest installment of his blockbuster movie franchise.

As much as she loved being surrounded by creative people who were excited to work with her, Tina was glad to be home. She walked through the house to get to the enclosed courtyard and noticed the servants were preparing the dining room for the dinner party. Tina was looking forward to celebrating her fifth wedding anniversary with a few close friends.

She stopped when she listened to the music wafting through the windows. It was the song from Dev's first hit movie. He only performed that dance for someone special. Tina hurried outside and along the stone path so she could watch.

She walked past the trees and her heart did a slow flip as she watched her lean and muscular husband holding their son close to his chest as he danced. Her heart did a slow flip as she watched Tanvir's little arms pump to the music as he gave a high-pitched laugh. Dev smiled, his harsh features softening as he completed the dance.

"Again!" Lakshmi, their daughter said, jumping up and down.

She watched Dev patiently teach Lakshmi an intricate step. Tina treasured moments like these. She placed her hand on her stomach, excited that their family continued to grow. She was nervous every time she became pregnant, but she trusted that Dev would be there when she needed him. He would do anything to protect her and their children.

Dev turned his head and captured her gaze. His eyes darkened with love and desire and she blushed when his mouth slanted into a wicked smile. She knew her children spotted her when she heard their squeals of delight. Tina raised her arms as the joy zipped through her veins.

She joined in and danced.

* * * * *

Mills & Boon® Hardback
April 2014

ROMANCE

A D'Angelo Like No Other	Carole Mortimer
Seduced by the Sultan	Sharon Kendrick
When Christakos Meets His Match	Abby Green
The Purest of Diamonds?	Susan Stephens
Secrets of a Bollywood Marriage	Susanna Carr
What the Greek's Money Can't Buy	Maya Blake
The Last Prince of Dahaar	Tara Pammi
The Sicilian's Unexpected Duty	Michelle Smart
One Night with Her Ex	Lucy King
The Secret Ingredient	Nina Harrington
Her Soldier Protector	Soraya Lane
Stolen Kiss From a Prince	Teresa Carpenter
Behind the Film Star's Smile	Kate Hardy
The Return of Mrs Jones	Jessica Gilmore
Her Client from Hell	Louisa George
Flirting with the Forbidden	Joss Wood
The Last Temptation of Dr Dalton	Robin Gianna
Resisting Her Rebel Hero	Lucy Ryder

MEDICAL

200 Harley Street: Surgeon in a Tux	Carol Marinelli
200 Harley Street: Girl from the Red Carpet	Scarlet Wilson
Flirting with the Socialite Doc	Melanie Milburne
His Diamond Like No Other	Lucy Clark

0314GEN STD HB

Mills & Boon® Large Print
April 2014

ROMANCE

Defiant in the Desert	Sharon Kendrick
Not Just the Boss's Plaything	Caitlin Crews
Rumours on the Red Carpet	Carole Mortimer
The Change in Di Navarra's Plan	Lynn Raye Harris
The Prince She Never Knew	Kate Hewitt
His Ultimate Prize	Maya Blake
More than a Convenient Marriage?	Dani Collins
Second Chance with Her Soldier	Barbara Hannay
Snowed in with the Billionaire	Caroline Anderson
Christmas at the Castle	Marion Lennox
Beware of the Boss	Leah Ashton

HISTORICAL

Not Just a Wallflower	Carole Mortimer
Courted by the Captain	Anne Herries
Running from Scandal	Amanda McCabe
The Knight's Fugitive Lady	Meriel Fuller
Falling for the Highland Rogue	Ann Lethbridge

MEDICAL

Gold Coast Angels: A Doctor's Redemption	Marion Lennox
Gold Coast Angels: Two Tiny Heartbeats	Fiona McArthur
Christmas Magic in Heatherdale	Abigail Gordon
The Motherhood Mix-Up	Jennifer Taylor
The Secret Between Them	Lucy Clark
Craving Her Rough Diamond Doc	Amalie Berlin

0314 GEN STD LP

Mills & Boon® Hardback
May 2014

ROMANCE

The Only Woman to Defy Him	Carol Marinelli
Secrets of a Ruthless Tycoon	Cathy Williams
Gambling with the Crown	Lynn Raye Harris
The Forbidden Touch of Sanguardo	Julia James
One Night to Risk it All	Maisey Yates
A Clash with Cannavaro	Elizabeth Power
The Truth About De Campo	Jennifer Hayward
Sheikh's Scandal	Lucy Monroe
Beach Bar Baby	Heidi Rice
Sex, Lies & Her Impossible Boss	Jennifer Rae
Lessons in Rule-Breaking	Christy McKellen
Twelve Hours of Temptation	Shoma Narayanan
Expecting the Prince's Baby	Rebecca Winters
The Millionaire's Homecoming	Cara Colter
The Heir of the Castle	Scarlet Wilson
Swept Away by the Tycoon	Barbara Wallace
Return of Dr Maguire	Judy Campbell
Heatherdale's Shy Nurse	Abigail Gordon

MEDICAL

200 Harley Street: The Proud Italian	Alison Roberts
200 Harley Street: American Surgeon in London	Lynne Marshall
A Mother's Secret	Scarlet Wilson
Saving His Little Miracle	Jennifer Taylor

0414GEN STD HB

Mills & Boon® Large Print
May 2014

ROMANCE

The Dimitrakos Proposition	Lynne Graham
His Temporary Mistress	Cathy Williams
A Man Without Mercy	Miranda Lee
The Flaw in His Diamond	Susan Stephens
Forged in the Desert Heat	Maisey Yates
The Tycoon's Delicious Distraction	Maggie Cox
A Deal with Benefits	Susanna Carr
Mr (Not Quite) Perfect	Jessica Hart
English Girl in New York	Scarlet Wilson
The Greek's Tiny Miracle	Rebecca Winters
The Final Falcon Says I Do	Lucy Gordon

HISTORICAL

From Ruin to Riches	Louise Allen
Protected by the Major	Anne Herries
Secrets of a Gentleman Escort	Bronwyn Scott
Unveiling Lady Clare	Carol Townend
A Marriage of Notoriety	Diane Gaston

MEDICAL

Gold Coast Angels: Bundle of Trouble	Fiona Lowe
Gold Coast Angels: How to Resist Temptation	Amy Andrews
Her Firefighter Under the Mistletoe	Scarlet Wilson
Snowbound with Dr Delectable	Susan Carlisle
Her Real Family Christmas	Kate Hardy
Christmas Eve Delivery	Connie Cox

Discover more romance at

www.millsandboon.co.uk

- ♥ WIN great prizes in our exclusive competitions

- ♥ BUY new titles before they hit the shops

- ♥ BROWSE new books and REVIEW your favourites

- ♥ SAVE on new books with the Mills & Boon® Bookclub™

- ♥ DISCOVER new authors

PLUS, to chat about your favourite reads, get the latest news and find special offers:

- Find us on facebook.com/millsandboon
- Follow us on twitter.com/millsandboonuk
- ♥ Sign up to our newsletter at millsandboon.co.uk